the

IMMORTAL
LOST

the

IMMORTAL LOST

THE PRIME IMMORTALS

H. R. PHILLIPS

TATE PUBLISHING & *Enterprises*

Published by Tate Publishing & Enterprises, LLC
127 E. Trade Center Terrace | Mustang, Oklahoma 73064 USA
1.888.361.9473 | www.tatepublishing.com

Tate Publishing is committed to excellence in the publishing industry. The company reflects the philosophy established by the founders, based on Psalm 68:11,
"The Lord gave the word and great was the company of those who published it."

Book design copyright © 2010 by Tate Publishing, LLC. All rights reserved.
Cover design by Kellie Southerland
Interior design by Lindsay B. Behrens

Published in the United States of America

ISBN: 978-1-61739-440-9
1. Fiction / Fantasy / Contemporary   2. Fiction / Fantasy / General
10.12.03

Acknowledgments

There are so many people whom I'd like to thank for making this book possible. First and foremost are my loving children, Dylan, Walker, Caleb, and Ella. Their wonderful imaginations have blessed me beyond expression.

I also have to say a very heartfelt thank you to my husband, family, and friends who have supported me through the years. I love you all.

A special thanks to Laurie Ann, who has always been my number one fan and best friend. Love you much, lady.

Last but not least, Cindy, thank you for being my support team. You are always there when I need you. So, my lovely Cindy, like you say after every email, "You can dance anywhere, even if only in your heart!"

Prologue

Our world, once a beautiful and lush planet, now struggles for survival. Where once there was life in abundance, it now dwindles. It is now a shell of its former self, dying at the hands of its inhabitants. It wasn't always so, before the days of black desolation. There was color in abundance and life blooming everywhere you looked.

A great civilization of advanced beings lived here alongside the human race, prospering before the destruction and oppressive weight of war. Entities from another world, they traveled from a planet lost to them and unknown to us, in search of a new beginning. It was the loss of their own beloved planet to war that had pushed the few who escaped its destruction to live in peace. They were scientists and explorers at heart. With their numbers so few, their search to create new life began. It was paramount for the survival of their species.

Capable of discovering and creating new life through science, they began their work on Earth alongside the human race. Hoping to cease the decline of their species, they began to experiment. Science brought life together, including species from their world, ours, and galaxies far away. They created and gave birth to an advanced life form. A species of life that was stronger in both mind and body. Never would they suffer from disease or natural death. Gifted with extraordinary abilities, the Immortals were born. Named the Prime, they flourished. Science reigned supreme, and the creators' way of life would continue to thrive through a new, stronger and healthier life form.

Only as some experiments do, they failed. They succeeded in creating life. Yet, with their creation, they brought destruction to us all. Scientists at heart, they had no idea the damage they had made. The Prime were strong both mentally and physically, as strong as their creators, but not without faults. As history has shown us time and time again, the strong shall conquer the weak. The Prime were no different.

A small faction calling themselves the Favored began to maneuver within the ranks for control and power. Once the Favored had gained the control they desired, they began wreaking havoc on any and all who would oppose their wishes. Time passed, and the Favored ruled with swift brutality over the land. Many suffered horrible treatment, yet the Favored continued to rule.

Only after years of abuse did a few finally rise up in protest, tired of the cruelty delivered by the Favored. Humans, creators, and the Prime came together, fighting back against the Favored, loath to be mistreated any longer. They fought, unwilling to be conquered. The once peaceful civilization coexisting with the human race was to be no more. The delicate balance was fractured, and the great wars began. Most of the Prime fled in the hopes of starting a new life. Yet others remained behind, protecting the human race. The Favored had to be stopped, and so the quest for Immortal domination began.

Twelve Immortal Prime families were chosen to stay behind and fight, led by the strongest and wisest of leaders, Alana. Their quest was to protect the unwitting human race from the Favored and bring peace back to the planet. Brothers and sisters in arms began waging war against their own. Against their own family members who had chosen to follow the dark side, becoming the ultimate lost. It was a time of death and destruction. Eventually battles were won and the Favored were sequestered and silenced, but not without losses. The chosen twelve had brought order back to the world, but at a very high price. Families were lost and enemies were made, but the majority of the Favored had been gathered and locked away in stasis, asleep to the world that had once been their playground of destruction. They were frozen in time, hidden away for what was considered to be their sentence, an eternity. They were never to be seen by immortal or mortal eyes again. Not until the day the creators returned. Yet some eluded capture and remain amongst us, hiding and waiting for the day they can avenge their fallen comrades.

For thousands of years, the Prime guardians stood vigil over the sentenced. Sentinels, watching over the imprisoned Favored and protecting humanity from the carnage that would surely ensue should they ever be awakened from slumber.

Whispers have begun to grow and strengthen, flying on the wind. Talk of an awakening is coming from sympathizers of the Favored. Dark forces entangled with the human race are growing, festering with hatred. Those who eluded capture now thrive in the dark arts, never forgetting the treachery of their creators and siblings.

Led by the one they call Abaddon, they hunt the remaining Prime guardians and their families, forcing them into the dark arts or killing them outright. The once peaceful are now at unrest.

Unprepared for the evil that grows all around them, the Prime guardians have no choice but to begin the gathering. The remaining four of the original twelve guardians search to locate Prime Immortals, those who were forgotten over time, entrusted to the human race. The Lost Ones, the offspring of the original twelve, are the only hope of restoring the delicate balance being threatened by the Favored and keeping peace amongst the races on Earth.

One

Dylan Black

"No! No, no, crap! Not now! Please don't do this to me now!" Disgusted, I slammed my hands against the steering wheel of the metallic blue Chevy Impala, looking to heavens and asking "Why me? Why does this always seem to happen to me?"

Shaking my head in dismay, I mentally cursed myself. I should have known better than to drive this old beast. It was on its last legs, or so Mack had said the last time I was home. I should have taken him up on his offer and bought the Honda Accord he had just finished rebuilding. Mentally, I berated myself for the second time. I needed to change my attitude and gain a little perspective. Hindsight was never good to dwell on. Looking to the heavens once more, I prayed Mack would be able to fix the old beast one more time, knowing that if anyone could fix the beast, it would be him.

I'd have to find a way to get the money to pay him for the repairs; if I was real lucky, he would have some work for me this summer and I could pay him that way.

I wasn't particularly religious, but I crossed myself as I had seen the nuns do so many times before on their pilgrimages to the reservation. I prayed for a little divine intervention. If it worked for them, why not give it a try? At this point, hope and faith were all I had.

After a rather hasty prayer, I snatched my old cell off the dash and quickly punched in the number to Mack's shop and waited. It rang once, then twice. Impatience was quickly taking over my fragile mental state. I could feel the panic beginning to grow, deep down inside of me. Opening the door of the old Chevy, I crawled out and leaned against the side of the blue monster, hating being stuck on the side of the road and waiting for someone to pick up the phone at Mack's Garage. After the fourth ring, that strange and disheartening feeling that I was all on my own began to get the better of me. Waiting was never one of my strong suits.

"Buck up, girl." Talking to myself, I pushed away from the side of the car and willed a little more backbone to show in my tired stride. I slowly paced the gravel road, while silently reprimanding myself for being so weak. Someone would eventually answer the phone. I just needed to be patient and have faith.

"Pick up!" Glancing at the heavens for the third time in less than a ten-minute period, I wondered if maybe I should have prayed for help to get home too. If someone didn't answer soon, who knows what would start running through my wild imagination.

With one foot tapping against the gravel road, I pulled the cell from my ear and checked the bars to see how much juice the battery had left. Noting that I was down to one and a half bars, I again prayed for someone, anyone, to pick up the phone. "Please pick up," I begged to no avail at the tenth ring. There was nothing but the continued ring on the other end. Slamming the phone shut with a little too much gusto, I worked the situation out in my mind.

The chances of someone being at the shop were pretty good, considering Mack lived just around the back side of the building in an old trailer that had been falling apart for over the last decade. Creature comforts were not something that Mack cared about, or so he said.

"As long as I have a place to lay my head at night out of the cold, baby girl, what else would a man need?" was the standard response received when asked by anyone about fixing up the old place or possibly getting a new mobile home.

I remembered back to one summer afternoon when I had completed all my work and decided, as a gift to Mack for his upcoming birthday, I would go clean and fix up the old place as much as I could. A woman's touch was what it needed, or in my case, a girl's touch. After walking into the small, cramped trailer, I had the overwhelming temptation to strike a match and watch it all go up in flames. Quickly calming my distraught nerves, I convinced myself that I wasn't in over my head. I would just take small steps. With one more cursory glance over the front room, I began to wish that I had gone shopping at the mall rather than attempt to take on such a daunting task. Shaking off any doubts or worries from my head, I rolled up my sleeves and got to work. Several hours later and completely exhausted, I had finished the job of mucking out the front rooms the best of my ability. I didn't make it past the living room area to the back bedrooms or bath, but the kitchen sparkled, and the little touches that I left behind made the small rooms homey. Mack would love it; and he did, for the short time it stayed that way.

A couple of weeks later, when I dropped by his trailer to give him a banana loaf that Mom and I had made, I had been shocked. I stood frozen just inside the door of Mack's little home, overcome with disappointment at seeing all the hard work that I achieved earlier completely gone. It was as if a tornado had gone through his living room and the dirty dish monster had set up camp in his kitchen; it was a mess, and I was devastated. What had once been a clean little home had reverted back to the filthy bachelor pad it had been before all my hard work. Mack's only reply to my unbelievable angst was, "Sorry, baby girl, you just can't teach an old dog new tricks."

Leaving his home upset and a little discouraged that he was never going to change, I swore that I would never again put myself out for him. I had been wrong, of course. The following day when Mack walked into the office and handed in some paperwork, he asked if I could grab his tool belt from his trailer. Still unhappy with him and with his request, I stood slowly, eventually moving to retrieve the missing tool belt from his manmade tornado-strewn trailer.

Happiness and pride were the emotions that rolled through me in waves after opening the exterior door of Mack's trailer and stepping inside his small home. After adjusting my eyes to the dimmer light in the room, I glanced around and felt immediate surprise. The once littered and messy little home was now clean and organized again. My eyes darted from the living room to the small kitchen; it sparkled. Just yesterday I had walked into a veritable pit of filth. Anger and disgust had overwhelmed me then; now it was gone, replaced by the knowledge that he had spent countless hours washing the mounds of dishes and picking up the old papers he had never gotten around to throwing away over the past weeks.

The living room was just as neat and clean; everything was in its place. The lap blanket that Mrs. Thundercloud, affectionately known as Mrs. T, had given him on his birthday was thrown delicately over the back of his old La-Z-Boy rocker. The pillows of the sofa were fluffed and the magazines stacked, but it was the sight of his end table that almost brought me to tears. Sitting directly in the center of the small table, between the remote control and the tacky touch lamp was a vase. A simple little vase, nothing special, one that had been salvaged from who knows where, that he had taken the time to fill with water and place beautiful wildflowers inside. Smiling, I took another quick glance around the small interior and located his tool belt next to the door in the now uncluttered entryway. Bending to grab it, I saw the little note lying on top. In Mack's very discernable handwriting, the words jumped from the scrap of paper.

"I guess this old dog is not that old."

That was it. He didn't need to say any more, I understood. Upon returning to the shop, I handed him the tool belt, smiling. I said nothing more than "Here you go, pup," and walked away. It was one of the best days I ever had that summer, and I will never forget it.

Flipping the phone open again, I punched the numbers one more time and prayed silently that someone would answer this time.

"Hello, Mack's Garage," a gravelly voice answered.

"Mack, thank God you're there. It's me, Dylan," I stated quickly.

"Dylan, baby girl, how you doing?" Mack said, excited to hear my voice; it had been a while since we had spoken. It was easy to recognize the happiness he felt at hearing my voice on the end of the line.

"Hey, Mack, I am doing great, but the beast has broken down, and I'm stuck on the highway about fourteen miles outside of town," I explained in an exhausted breath. "Could you please send Ty out to pick me up?"

"Sure, baby girl, he's already on his way."

I could hear Ty in the background shout, "No problem; be there in ten."

"Thanks, Mack." Relief swam through my body, and I felt the tension I had been holding onto for the past half hour draining away.

"No problem, baby girl. Are you home for a short visit or planning on staying awhile?" Mack asked, in his not-so-subtle manner.

"Yeah, I am home for a visit, just not sure for how long. I guess we'll just have to see what the fates have in store for the beast and I." Knowing that I would be moving into the city in two weeks but hating to disappoint him over the phone, I would wait to discuss the job situation until I could explain it to him in person.

Hinting at the fact that I would like him to take a look at the old beast and praying that it was still fixable, I asked. "Do you got a lot going on, Mack?" while wishing the shop wasn't real busy and knowing deep down that it probably was.

"Busy enough, baby girl. We'll just have to see how the old beast is doing before we let you head out again, now won't we?" I could hear the smile on his face and the wheels turning in his head as he spoke, knowing all too well that the beast would not be top priority on the list of to do's for Mack. I would not be leaving town any time soon.

"I don't suppose you still have that Honda Accord you rebuilt last time I was back? It was in your yard when I left." I questioned him hopefully, knowing full well that the chance of it still being in the yard was slim to none.

Mack was the best mechanic in town, and as far as I knew the best mechanic within four counties. If he had a car on his lot for sale, it didn't take long for someone to snatch it up.

"Sorry, baby girl, she sold a couple of days after I put the for sale sign on her."

"Not surprised by that one." Sighing, I continued. "Are you working on anything now?" I questioned him with nervous anticipation, feeling myself holding onto my breath while waiting for his answer.

"Maybe, we'll talk when you get here. Ty should be there shortly, and I have a customer I need to get to. See you in a bit, baby girl." I heard the click of the receiver, and he was gone.

"Okay, Mack, bye!" I was a little frustrated after hearing the silence on the other end of the now dead cell phone. His quick dismissal to my question was upsetting; it wasn't like Mack to be so short with me; after all, I was his baby girl. Remembering back to the day when I received the loving nickname made me strangely uncomfortable.

Ryer and Willow, twins and older by a full six years, had walked me to the general store the first afternoon I met Mack.

Thinking to myself, I placed my cell phone into the front pocket of my Aero hoodie and climbed up onto the hood of the beast. Making myself as comfortable as I possibly could while I waited for Ty to show up. I reminisced about that day with mixed feeling. Remembering every little detail I could. It was the first time I had been allowed to go into town without one of my parents at my side. It had also been the first time I ever had a vision or picture story, like I used to call them, with such dark power.

The only reason I had gotten to go to town that day was because my mom had discovered that I had been doing my siblings' chores. Ryer and Willow would frequently ask me for help with their chores because of how quickly I was able to complete them. The fact that I could accomplish so much in such a short period of time allowed for more time to play or create great adventures that we would all go on.

I didn't mind the work; it was fun for me, giving me something to do with my siblings. Meda, my adoptive mother, did not see it the same way. She didn't agree with Ryer and Willow pushing their chores off onto the smallest family member's tiny hands, then expecting to still reap the rewards of their non-existent laboring. No, they were not going to get away without having to pay for their laziness. After all, they were being paid an allowance for the chores that they completed, not what I had completed for them. For them to reap the rewards, when it was my working hands that had completed the chores, angered Mom. "Life is not free, and you two should know that expecting someone to carry your weight in life will get you nowhere." Mom had been very upset with Ryer and Willow for taking advantage of me. I had gone to bat for them, protesting that I didn't mind the work, explaining that I thought it was fun. I told her it wasn't like working to me. The fact that it had been fun didn't matter to Mom. They needed to be taught a lesson, and she wanted me to fall in line.

"Oh, *ciqala*." She lovingly held my hand and bent to looked into my eyes. She always called me by the Sioux name meaning "small child" when she was feeling overly protective. "You are too sweet, but your brother and sister must learn responsibility. Completing their chores for them takes away all of the responsibility I try to give them." Taking a deep breath, she stood and looked to me as if she was a little disappointed in my reaction to being taken advantage of. Directing her attention to the now thoroughly chastised duo standing before her, she explained their punishment.

"Since your sister does not feel that doing your chores is a burden, and she is more than happy to do them for you, she will be the only one receiving an allowance this week." I watched as the smile crossed her face and the glee in her eyes sparkled when Ryer and Willow started to complain. Holding her hand up and silently requesting the floor again, she stated "Unless, of course, you would like to receive your allowance by helping me in the kitchen, Willow." Turning her now happy face to Ryer, she continued, "You could also gain some allowance by weeding the garden for me, Ryer." Another smile crossed her lips, and I could tell that she was extremely happy with herself and her next thought process. "Of course, you will also need to pay young Dylan for the service that she performed for you as well." The shouting began again, and Mom's hand went up for a second time, silencing the twins effectively.

"Dear little Dylan, how would you like to be paid for your services today?" she asked with anticipation. I could see that she had a precise thought rolling in her mind that would be sufficient for the payment, but didn't know for sure. So I closed my eyes and pulled her thoughts to me in a vision. As it always had in the past, with anyone who I wanted to understand better, I would reach into their thoughts and come back with pictures. I couldn't always understand what the pictures meant, and sometimes I got confused about what it was that I was seeing; but after a while, I got rather good at deciphering them. I could tell what people were thinking and what they wanted. It was easiest with Mom, as if I was tuned into what she was thinking at all times. I would know what she was planning on wearing that day or if she needed something while she was cleaning or cooking; it was just natural with her. With others I had to try a little harder, but eventually I would come away with something. I could look at people in the store and determine what purchase they would be making before they could even place it in their cart. It was a game, one that I played to pass the time as my mother did her shopping.

The day I stopped randomly pulling information from people's heads was the day I saw him—a stranger who had just stopped on his way through town. He was an average-looking man, with dark blonde hair and a slight build. There was really nothing at all menacing about him. I had just finished pulling the last shopping item from old Mr. Jacobs's head and was giggling to myself at the thought of him having to put glue on his teeth to keep them in.

When the dark blonde stranger began walking up the aisle toward me, I turned to face him fully and began to probe. The pictures that I received were strange. I didn't understand at first what it was that I was seeing, but I knew they were coming from his thoughts, of that much I was sure. He was there in the pictures along with another man, and they were fighting. There was a lot of anger, and I could see that the other man was scared. They continued to argue, and then there was a flash of light. Then everything changed and the pain came. A sharp, stabbing pain assaulted my entire being, searing every nerve ending within my body. I fell to the floor and began screaming "Stop, stop!" Rolled in a tight little ball on the cold floor of the shopping center, I clutched my head with one hand and hugged my side with the other, praying for the pain to stop. Tears streamed down my face, and I shook violently, pleading for it to end.

Mom fell to her knees, grabbing hold of my small form and tightly hugging me to her chest. She questioned me while struggling to figure out what was happening. I let go of my head and grasped her arm, continuing to cry and pleading for relief. Slowly I raised my other arm with the last bit of strength I possessed toward the crowd of people who had begun to surround us. With my hand extended, I pointed to the man with the dark blonde hair.

"Make him stop, Mom; make him stop." Mom glanced over the small crowd now gathered by my commotion and landed her gaze upon the dark blonde stranger. Immediately she knew she needed to leave. Picking up my fragile body, we rushed from the store and hurried home.

It was later that evening, when both my parents were watching the news that I discovered what exactly had happened in the store that day. I was supposed to be tucked into bed, but sleep would not come. In order to get my mother to leave my bedroom, I had to pretend to be asleep. She had been very upset over my outburst at the store, and it had been extremely difficult to convince her that I was all right. Every time I had a strong vision or picture I had spoken to her about it, but not this time. I couldn't explain this one to her, not without scaring her completely. Truth be told, I really didn't want to see again what he had shown me in his mind that day. I was tired, and my whole body was exhausted at the effort it took to stop the pain.

Once I had convinced her that I was soundly asleep, I waited for her to return downstairs before sitting up and attempting to eavesdrop on their conversation. I could hear them speaking, and I could feel the worry in both of my parents' minds. I was only getting bits and pieces of what they were thinking and saying. My mind was too wrapped up in what I had experienced earlier that day. All my thoughts from the day were flashing through my mind. With super speed they whipped through my mind. It was difficult to control them. Sifting though each one was quite a process, but I picked out the thoughts I was looking for and considered them. After a short period of time had passed, I could hear my parents hushed voices and thoughts as they discussed the news on TV. They were talking about a story that my father had just seen broadcast.

A local businessman had been murdered. According to the headlines, he had been shot by his business partner over a deal gone bad. The suspect in the case had been apprehended not but fifteen miles outside of town. My parents suspected immediately that the events of the day might be related, but I knew then that the suspect or murder they were referring to was indeed the same man who had given his thoughts to me in the store. I didn't sleep at all that night, and it would be several nights before I was able to close my eyes without seeing the murder of the businessman in my sleep.

I had come to the conclusion on one of those sleepless nights that it wasn't safe to play my picture game anymore. I began to shove the pictures away from my consciousness to the back of my mind, locking down the hurt and hiding the terrifying pictures that left me lying awake in bed at night, unable to sleep. They had to be stopped, put away, and never seen again. The only problem with that was I would no longer be myself. No longer would I be the carefree child who could pick a picture out of a random person's thought and happily share its joy with the sender. I had changed. I was withdrawn into myself, completely losing the child that I was, until it was no longer easy for my mom to look at me and understand. Where had her little girl gone? After a very stressful day of blocking thoughts and visions, I had become irritated with my surroundings and was acting out quite shamefully. It was then she took me aside and explained the only way she knew how. Holding me on her lap, she spoke softly, stroking my arms, gently rocking, and carefully hushing my disturbed emotions.

"Dylan, some of us are born with gifts." she said softly. "You have been blessed with the vision of life."

"I don't want it!" I had protested.

"You may not want it now, after all that has happened, but it has already been given to you by the gods, and it cannot be given back." Mom explained.

I hung my head and began to pout. "What if I gave it to Willow? She could have it if she wants it; that wouldn't be giving it back to the gods!" I cried.

"I am sorry, my sweet; this is your gift to bear. And besides, Willow has her own gift. Right now you are upset, but the gods gave you this gift for a reason." I continued to cry as she pulled me tighter to her chest, hugging and rocking me while wishing away my pain.

After I had poured out all the tears my small frame could, she turned me around and slowly began to explain to me the gift I had been blessed with. When I had heard all she had to say, I removed myself from her lap and began to walk away. She grabbed my arm and held me in place, knowing I was still unsure.

"Remember, Dylan, if used properly, you could help those in need; now is that not a great gift from the gods?" I had smiled, nodded my head in confirmation, and silently walked to my room. I had decide that day, even after hearing all that my mother had said in the comfort of her arms, that if the gods had given this gift to me and if I couldn't give it back, I would need to be very careful with it so as not to be hurt by it again. That meant there would be no more playing the picture game with people. Not with friends, neighbors, teachers, strangers, or even my family. I would continue to hide it. Every time I would feel a thought coming from someone I would push it away, locking it down somewhere deep in the corners of my mind. I would concentrate on something else, like math, searching for complex equations and seeing complicated problems pop up instead of people's thoughts.

In the beginning it was difficult. I struggled to keep the pictures away, only to feel them crawling up into my consciousness as if they had a life of their own. It was months before I was able to walk through a store with Mom and not feel the telltale signs of people's thoughts and pictures encroaching into my own vision. Eventually, I succeeded in removing everyone's thoughts, with the exception of my mom. She was the only person I couldn't block out. It was different with her. I didn't feel violated by her thoughts. I felt safe, and I knew when I looked at the pictures in her mind, I would be okay.

So the day Mom had gazed at me and asked the question as to what I wanted for payment, it had been easy to see her thoughts. The pictures had popped into my head and a smile grew on my face. Instantly I knew what I wanted, and I also knew why she had chosen that particular thought.

Earlier that day I had been begging her to do just what her thoughts were suggesting I do with my siblings, and so I pronounced my fee for all to hear and watched as the storm began to show in Willow's eyes.

"I would like to walk to the store and have an ice cream, please." I smiled so hard that my face felt like it would crack. I stared at my mom, and she smiled brightly back at me, knowing I had tapped into her thoughts; she was pleased with the outcome.

"As you wish, my sweet." She turned to Willow and Ryer. "You heard her. For payment of the chores she has completed for you, you will take your little sister to the store. With your own money, you will purchase her the ice cream of her choice."

Willow was not pleased; she began to whine immediately. "Mom that is not fair…I…" She stopped short when Mom quickly raised her hand, halting her protests.

Mom continued, "After you have made the purchase of ice cream for your sister, you will sit with her until she has completed eating it and then walk her home. Do you understand?" She looked pointedly at both her older children, willing them to not protest. She would not tolerate an argument and was tired of listening to the complaining.

I observed as a defeated Willow hung her head and stated that she understood. Ryer stood nodding his head, as if it was no big deal and began walking toward the door. I yelled after him to wait and he did. Willow, on the other hand, had stomped out the door and sulked her way up the drive. I raced after Ryer and grabbed his hand; together we walked slowly behind a very angry Willow, making sure not to get in the line of her sight. Ryer was Willow's twin, and they were best friends most of the time, inseparable when they were younger. But recently Willow had been changing, spending more time with girls her own age and leaving Ryer to hang with his buddies more and more.

At home, Willow would ignore both Ryer and me, choosing to talk on the phone or write in her journal. So Ryer and I began spending more time with each other, and eventually he allowed me to tag along with his buddies and be their mascot, of sorts. I understood why Willow didn't want me going to the store with her that day. She thought that I was a baby and that I said too much to her friends when I was around them about stuff that I shouldn't know. But that was before, when I would see the pictures in their heads and asked questions as to why they thought some boy was so cute or other unusual things that teenage girls thought. I didn't do that anymore. Instead of pushing the already angry Willow by walking next to her, I conceded to stroll behind with Ryer at my side.

Willow and Ryer would regularly go to the little general store and buy ices from Mrs. Whitetail. Her daughter, Snow, was Willow's best friend, and they used to play all the time together until recently, when Tommy Olsted decided that Willow was prettier than Snow and asked her to the Season Fling. Willow had said no, of course, but the asking had been done and Snow was very upset. She blamed Willow for stealing her boyfriend and ruining her life. I didn't understand why she was so upset, and Ryer was no help in explaining it. I guess at thirteen years old, it was a big deal; I just don't remember having the same problems when I turned thirteen. Then again, I never had the abundance of friends that Willow had been blessed with.

The results of Tommy's actions had a ripple effect and poor Willow had lost several of her friends over it. It didn't help her status in the friend department to have a little sister who was capable of pulling thoughts and visions from their heads and verbalizing them. No, Willow didn't have many friends left, and the few she did were not her best friend, Snow. She hadn't spoken to Snow in almost a month, and Mom was getting very worried about her. It was just yesterday Mom had an argument over Willow going to the store and picking up a few things.

"Mom, please, can't Ryer go?" Willow pleaded. "You can't expect me to go there. Snow will be working behind the counter, and she will just ignore me again." Willow's face hung, and you could see the defeat and hurt in her eyes.

Gently Mom folded Willow into her arms and assured her that all would be forgotten. "She will come around, Willow. When Snow realizes that she has a good friend in you, all will be well."

I went to comfort her as well, placing a hand on her shoulder and gently sliding it down her arm. "Snow is your friend. She will come around, just like Mom says she will." I waited for a response, but nothing came. "If you want, you can tell her that I won't hang around and pester you all anymore; maybe that would make her happy." That had done it; she smiled and punched my arm. It didn't hurt, but Ryer had still been the one to go to the store for the supplies that day.

As we approached the store that afternoon, Willow slowed her steps and waited for us to catch up. Most of the steam from her earlier anger was gone, and she was more apprehensive as we approached the store, not knowing what awaited her inside. Letting go of Ryer's hand, I quickly grabbed hers and gave a gentle squeeze. This would be the first time she had seen Snow in weeks, and she was nervous. I smiled up at her and willed her all my strength. She smiled, squeezed my hand gently, and proceeded to follow Ryer into the store with me in tow.

Walking up to the counter hand-in-hand where Snow was working with her mother, we ordered our ice cream from Mrs. Whitetail and watched as she went to the back of the room to retrieve them from the larger freezer. Snow stood quietly, trying very hard to avoid eye contact with Willow. Willow was doing the same, attempting to act nonchalant while reading a magazine from the rack next to the register. It was tense, and no one was comfortable, with the exception of Ryer; he was oblivious to the situation unfolding. I found out years later that boys at that age usually were.

We watched as Mrs. Whitetail came from the back of the room with three ice cream bars in her hands, ready to be distributed to her waiting customers. It was very obvious when she elbowed Snow in the side and asked her to deliver them to us that she was anxious to see reconciliation between the two girls. Snow approached the counter after taking the ice cream from her mother's grasp. First, she looked to me and gently placed one in my very eager hand with a smile. I returned the smile with honest gratitude and said a very warm "thank you." She then turned to Ryer, handing him the second one. Being caught up in "guy stuff" as he called it, he sometimes forgot his manners and almost forgot to say thank you, until I elbowed him in the ribs.

As a result of my deliberate prodding, a very speedy "thanks!" shot out of his mouth before he turned, disappearing down an aisle to look for the latest hotrod magazines. I watched as Snow followed him with her eyes and shouted after him, "No, thank you!"

I was a little confused by her comment, as was Willow, if the expression on her face was any clue. I watched as Snow turned back around and walked toward Willow. It took me a moment, but I figured it out after I saw Ryer peeking over the racks in the aisle directly behind Snow. With Snow's back turned away from him and Willow staring directly at Snow, I smiled and understood that this was a fix.

Snow extended her hand and gave Willow the last ice cream. Stepping a little closer, she placed her hand on Willow's shoulder and whispered, "I'm sorry." That was all it took. Willow and Snow were the best of friends again, as if the past month had never happened and Tommy had never asked the hated question. Life just picked up where it had left off over a month ago. I never understood the dynamics of the teenage girl years, even with having to go through them myself, but as long as Willow was happy, that was all that mattered.

I had just finished my ice cream and was ready to go when Willow, who had been hovering by the front counter talking to Snow, walked over. She gave Ryer's arm a squeeze and told him that she loved him under her breath. He flinched and walked away, ignoring the sentiment.

"You guys go on ahead and tell Mom that I will be home later for dinner, I am going to stay and help Snow out with a few of her chores." Willow smiled a huge smile and skipped over to where Snow and her mother were standing in the front part of the storage room.

Ryer tapped my shoulder to get my attention and said, "Okay, kid, I guess it is just you and me for the rest of the afternoon. Could you stand walking to the junkyard to see if they have a bike chain for the monster?"

I knew he could feel my excitement when he quickly followed his last statement with "This has to be our secret; you know how Mom gets when you go too far from home. She would be very angry if she knew, so no telling, okay?" He covered his lips with his finger while simultaneously shushing me and rubbing my head.

Whispering as softly as I could while making sure he still heard me, I nodded my head and said, "I promise."

Ryer and I were walking the six additional blocks to the junkyard; we had already passed several of our neighbors on Main Street. Mr. Talbot was just walking out of the hardware store with his cat, Percy, walking on a leash. He had the only cat that I had ever seen with three legs.

Mrs. Janis was pushing her third baby down the sidewalk with the other two trailing behind, no doubt heading for the general store we had just come from. I liked her daughter, Carry. She was a very sweet girl. We used to play with each other quite a bit before I scared her at school one day by telling her the stories in her head. Now Mrs. Janis walks to the other side of the road when she sees us coming.

I cried for a whole day when I was told I could no longer play with Carry. Her mother preferred that I not come to the afternoon play sessions in their home for the younger girls in our neighborhood. I didn't understand at the time. According to what she said to my mom, she was only trying to protect her daughter from what she felt was a "bad influence."

Mom had returned her comment with, "Mrs. Janis, you have no imagination, and without it you will be sorely pressed for greatness." She hung up the phone and held my weeping little body close to her chest. "Ciqala, please don't worry, all will be well. You'll see; they will come around." I wondered who she was trying to convince more, me or herself.

Later that evening I asked Ryer and Willow what a "bad influence" was. They said it was just something people like Carry's mom said when they didn't know what else to say. I still didn't understand, but I heard it in Ryer's head that Carry's mom was stupid. He was angry with her and I was still confused.

Ryer and Willow had made up for the loss of my friends by playing with me as much as they could. Of course, I always had my mom to keep me busy. It didn't take long and soon I had forgotten all about the fact I was being dubbed a "bad influence." But it was never the same for me at school.

I rarely had friends to play with, so the majority of the time I would study. Solving math problems in my head and breaking down equations without putting them to paper was a challenge, and I liked it. I had hoped I would have friends as Mom said I would, but it never really worked out that way.

Ryer and I had gone almost four blocks; we were walking around the corner of Main Street and stepping onto Maple Avenue. The junkyard wasn't much farther; with only two more blocks to go, we would be there shortly. Little did I know what would happen before we got there.

Two

Dylan

The excitement was overwhelming. I had never been this far away from home without one of my parents. I was only seven at the time, and it had been established by my over-caring parents that I was too young to "run the town," as they put it.

As we approached our destination, I started to feel something curious, a strange yet familiar sensation. The excitement I had been feeling just moments before flew from my body, replaced now with almost a sense of dread or warning. I didn't understand where it was coming from. We had just made it past Minnie's Hair Salon when I felt the sensation becoming stronger. Now it felt as if I was being watched and someone was making sure I knew it.

Stopping, I stood completely still, trying to determine what this feeling was and why it seemed so familiar. That's when I remembered last year, right before my sixth birthday, the same feeling overtook me. At the time my mother was there and with her strong arms around me, it had disappeared quickly. This time she was absent and the feeling was growing stronger. Someone or something was angry and it was watching me. I could feel the hate. Whoever it was, was not happy with me at all.

Suddenly explosions of light clouded my eyes. I couldn't see. Clutching my head and squeezing my eyes tightly shut, I willed it to stop.

Then he was there, the man in black with scary eyes. He was coming for me! I snapped my eyelids open, scanning the area all around me, searching. I couldn't see him, but he was there, just out of sight; I was sure of it. I could feel his fury toward me grow in strength as I shivered and waited for something to happen.

Whipping my head from one direction to the other, I searched everywhere to see who he was and where he was coming from.

Finally, I felt him moving near me, angry and hateful. I could feel the hostility rolling off him towards me. Frozen in place, I stood waiting to see him, the man whom I had glimpsed behind my closed eyes, but he was not there.

I closed my eyes again and he appeared before me, just at the end of the street. I watched as he said something in a language I didn't understand. Unable to absorb his words, I stood still, frozen in place and waiting for something, anything, to happen. I may not have understood what his words meant, but there was no confusing his intent. He was coming for me.

In the back of my mind I could hear the faint sound of Ryer speaking to me. He was saying something. I wasn't sure what it was. I was so afraid. Clouded by the feelings coming from the stranger, I slowly and reluctantly opened my eyes and turned to see Ryer still moving down the sidewalk.

After what seemed to be an eternity, I began to hear his words. He was in front of me, trying to coax me along, saying something like, "Come on, slow-poke!" Yes, he was trying to get me to move, but my feet were heavy and wouldn't budge, as if they were stuck in the prairie gumbo. I thought about asking for help, but before I could say anything Ryer caught the expression of terror on my face and began to walk back to where I stood motionless.

I looked to the heavens, and the sky began to change from the beautiful, sunny day we had been enjoying just minutes earlier to a dark, cloud-covered, cold, rank-smelling afternoon. Clouds raced across the sky as if they were running from the day. The gentle breeze that had been there earlier turned into an ice whipped wind that was shocking as it pelted the skin.

Ryer had almost made it back to where I stood silent on the sidewalk. He looked concerned, or maybe it was confusion along with irritation at me for slowing down our progress, I wasn't sure. He seemed to be fine; as if he couldn't see or feel what was happening all around us. It was as if he was completely oblivious to what I was seeing and feeling. As if he didn't know that a man dressed in black with hateful eyes was standing directly behind us, with fury exuding from his very pores. Something horrible was about to happen, couldn't Ryer see that?

I could feel the panic bubbling up into my chest, and then when I felt I could stand no more, the dark man was there. His mouth was moving; he was speaking to me, but this time I couldn't hear him. The wind was taking his words away faster than they could reach me.

I studied him intently, wondering who he was and why his anger was directed at me. He was dressed in darkness, cloaked from top to bottom. He was as dark as the crows that sat in my mother's backyard, ignoring the scarecrow that should have kept them away from our precious garden. He looked every bit as ominous as those screeching birds with the sharp black beaks.

His long, shiny black hair was tied in a braid down his back. A few strands had escaped the leather band, only to be whipped in the icy cold wind around his rage-filled face. He was tall and very well built, that much was obvious. I could see it in the apparent strength he presented, from his well-corded arms down to his clenching fists and then to sturdy muscled legs, encased in black leather. He stood over six feet tall and exuded a menacing aurora of death all about him.

Shivering, I could feel his hate; it covered me like a creeping vine, pulling tighter and tighter, trying to strangle the life from my body. A cloak covered his shoulders and cascaded down his back, blowing in the wind, only adding more mystery to the menace that lay beneath its cover. Wrapping my arms around my body in the hopes of comforting myself against his wrath, I prayed for him to leave and never return, only to discover that no amount of comfort or praying would stop the pain that was beginning to form behind my eyes. The understanding that he would never leave willingly hung in the air, making it difficult to breathe.

I watched as he moved his hand slowly from his side, placing its weight on the hilt of the dagger lashed to his waist. I couldn't move my eyes from the sight of his fingers curling around its wickedness. I was afraid to look away; I stared.

Strangely, looking at the dagger sheathed and strapped to his side, I knew the undeniable truth of its existence. I knew that its deadly cold steel, ancient as it was, had been honed for one purpose only—killing and nothing more. Time and again it had been used in battle, wielded against those he deemed his enemy and any who had the nerve to disobey him. Sickened at the knowledge of what my mind was absorbing from him, I forced myself to look away from the dagger. Only then did I realize my mistake.

His entire being screamed evil, but it wasn't until I looked into his eyes that I understood; they were dark black, void of emotion, cold, unforgiving, dead. I searched his face, hoping to understand his anger with me. He spoke again, and his words were carried away from me on the wind once more. Then unexpectedly he smiled, an ominous smile, and drew the dagger from his side. I watched as he took steps toward me, moving closer with each footfall, then he stopped. Something or someone had stopped him. He was furious, and he shouted against the wind that was now swirling fiercely around him, holding him at bay. I couldn't see who or what was stopping him, but I could feel the strength in them. Just as suddenly as the wind and darkness had appeared, so did the light. It happened so quickly, as if a lightning bolt struck me, awakening my entire being to the surroundings that had shocked me into silent stillness. Now more aware of my body and the fact that I was in danger, I took flight. Energy raced through me, giving strength to the limbs that had been paralyzed with fear moments earlier.

I was running as fast as my feeble legs could take me, darting glances back to see where the man in black was and how much time I had before he eventually caught me in his iron grip.

Each glimpse behind me showed nothing of the man in black; all I could see was the swirling remnants of dark black sky where he once stood. He was nowhere to be seen, but he was still there; I could feel him. A horrible feeling that his icy grip would reach me spurred me on. He may be fast, but I would be faster. *Run!* My mind screamed; the wind was cold against the bare skin of my arms and legs, its chill whirling around me, pelting tiny shards of ice against my small form. The wind's bite exhausted me quicker than the pace of my own feet. He was still behind me, gaining ground, and I was tired, yet I continued to run. I couldn't give up or slow down; he was right behind me, hunting his prey. I needed to keep going. *Faster!* I prayed to the heavens that my feet would carry me like the wind. Taking another quick look behind me, I risked everything to see if he was still there. He wasn't. I sensed him, but all I could see was the dark sky and the cold fog where he had once stood. Where was he?

Salty tears streamed down my cheeks, staining my face and making it difficult to see. The sound of my heart pounding against my chest vibrated in my ears, deafening any other sound to my eardrums. I was afraid. I had to move faster; I could feel him catching up with me! I pushed my exhausted legs even harder; my lungs were on fire, and it was becoming difficult to breath. Was he going to catch me?

In the distance I could hear Ryer's voice; he was yelling at me to stop, but I couldn't. I wanted to scream at him to run, but I couldn't find my voice. Then the man in black had me. With his cold deathly viselike hands, he grasped my weary body.

I closed my eyes and started thrashing, hoping to disengage myself from his hold. "No! Let me down! Let me down!" I screamed. His grip only got stronger, and I could feel the air being wrung from my lungs like a wet washcloth. This was it; he had me. I squeezed my eyes tightly shut and prayed for strength. My tired legs continued to beat weakly against the iron body of my captor. I could feel the energy seeping from my bones and knew I couldn't hold on for much longer. With my eyes closed so that I wouldn't see the strike of the dagger, I gave in. Defeated, he would finish me off. It was the sound of my own weak voice, desperately seeking strength one last time. My own voice telling me this would not be the end. I couldn't give up. I needed to fight. Digging deep inside,

I gathered what little strength I had left. I could feel it building, growing within me, slowly at first and then in a rush of strength, exploding through out me.

"*No!*" Not like this. I fought, screaming and kicking with every inch of my being; blow after blow I hammered at my captor. I wasn't going to die, not like this.

With my eyes still closed, I pummeled him with every ounce of strength I had in me. I could hear Ryer's voice yelling, "Stop it, Dylan! Please stop!"

Suddenly, like a light switch being turned on, I felt the presence of peace. It warmed the air and surrounding me with it essence. Peace was pushing away the darkness and replacing the icy cold grasp with warmth and light.

The darkness was leaving; it was letting go. The frigid cold was creeping away slowly, losing the battle against the warmth that surrounded me. Unwilling to admit defeat, an animal growl came from the man in black; he would not be defeated so easily. He was angry, enraged; and then as if he had been there all along, he was in my mind. I watched as he smiled, seething, trying to hold his grasp on me, trying and failing. His whole body flexed in anger, and he looked to the last of the darkened sky and bellowed his fury. Anger rolled off his body and saturated the air around him; he had lost, and he knew it.

His dark, cold eyes stared though me. Contorting his face into an ugly smile, he began to laugh. I shivered as he pierced the air with the sound of his cold and heartless cackle. The exposed flesh of my arms crawled with the fear he invoked inside me. Finally, his laughter ceased and he spoke. He wanted to strike fear inside of me, and he did exactly that with only a few words. "You will not always be so lucky, collector. Another day, another time, I will finish you."

Trembling with fright, I watched as he slowly turned and disappeared from my mind.

Shaking with the terror he had instilled inside of me, I battled for control of my body. The sting of what felt like ice running though my veins, had not stopped when he had finally turned, disappearing from my mind. It wasn't over. I knew instinctively that even though he wasn't with me presently, he would never really be gone. With the dread of his words lingering in my mind, my body continued to fight. He had warned that I wouldn't be so lucky the next time our paths crossed. I prayed for strength, while fighting to fill my lungs. My breath was coming hard, and I labored to gain just a minute amount of oxygen to fill them. With the faint grip of darkness still surrounding me, I pulled in a deep breath and grasped for more. I could feel the darkness getting weaker. Opening my mouth, I sucked in another deep gulp, allowing my lungs to fill completely. The icy fear that had consumed me was slowly letting go. The strength in my body was returning, and I could feel the weight of fear lifting. I was confused. What was happening? I could hear Ryer's voice again.

"Dylan, stop, stop!" I could hear the fear in his voice. The darkness was falling away, the cold dissipating. Where was I?

I was suspended in the air; I could feel strong arms holding me and for a second I thought he was back. I began to thrash once again, hoping that he would drop me. Ryer's voice came to me again. "Dylan, please stop!"

Seconds passed before I understood what was happening. The darkness was gone; I was okay. Someone was holding me, cradling my small form against the warmth of his body.

I had no fight left; I was exhausted. Another gulp of air, and I could hear Ryer saying, "It's okay! Dylan, you're okay." With my body heavy and slowly relaxing, I leaned more fully into the strength of the body that surrounded me. It was warm and comforting, nothing like that of the man in black.

Exhausted and barely able to open my eyes, I grasped what little energy I had left and willed them open. A slight fluttering of lashes, and I was looking into a pair of golden brown eyes staring back at me with confusion and concern. They were not Ryer's, but they were very similar in color.

With my eyes quivering shut again, I relaxed and concentrated on the heat flowing through my body. Warmth was chasing away the darkness, filling my limbs and pushing the last bit of coldness from me.

With my eyes closed, I concentrated on the new pictures that gathered in my head. They were better now, not as scary. I could feel the worry and concern Ryer had for me. I could see his face; he was upset, scared really. Not because of the cold darkness like me, but more concerned for what I was obviously going through. I could see the stress and feel his concern for both himself and me.

Was he going to be in trouble? It was the question that kept crossing his mind along with the prayer that he kept repeating, "Please let her be okay. Please let her be okay." I felt badly for him.

The bitter darkness was gone, and so was the man in black with the hateful eyes. I was fine and knew that all I needed to do was open my eyes. Before I could open them, the pictures in my mind changed. Tall grass was blowing in the wind, beautiful mountains were on the horizon, and I could hear a voice. She was singing, speaking to me, "Follow your heart, Dylan; come to me." The voice on the wind just kept repeating it, over and over again. It was beautiful. The darkness had been replaced.

The sound of her voice was pulling at me. Following it, I crested a small hillside and stood silent, listening. Standing alone on top of the hill with a gentle breeze blowing though my hair, I was at peace.

It was beautiful. There were green, lush foothills below snow-capped mountains. The sky was clear, and I could smell the fragrant scent of wild flowers. With sunshine all around me, I quietly stood and listened for the voice, the sound of the angel who had been speaking to me. She was there, just out of reach—a shimmering vision of light in the lush beauty that lay before me.

Her voice came to me again, stronger this time, and she began to take form. She was blindingly beautiful. Golden flowing hair cascaded down her back and danced in the wind. Angelic, she was dressed in an iridescent gown of rainbow colors that played in the sunlight.

Her loving green eyes caressed me from head to toe; softly she spoke, "Come to me, Dylan."

I wanted to go to her. I stepped forward, moving into her waiting arms, but no sooner did I do so, than she began to disappear. She was leaving, her voice fading, absorbed by the wind that had quickly picked up and began lifting her away.

I begged her not to leave. "Please, don't go!" I pleaded, attempting to take another step forward into her quickly evaporating arms, only to watch as the last glimmer of her vanished from view. All that was left was the faint sound of her voice being carried on the wind, farther and farther away. Finally, there was nothing left but empti-ness. I was alone!

"*No!*" I screamed. My eyes flew open, and I was aware of someone holding me. I grabbed tightly to the material of his shirtfront, not willing to let it go. My eyes slammed shut, and the tears flowed freely as I clung to the man holding me. He smelled of motor oil and gasoline, but at that moment, he was my lifeline and the only hope of survival I felt I had.

Slowly, reality began to sink in. I heard voices around me. Ryer was speaking with another man, not the one presently holding me in his embrace. As my tears began to slow, their voices became clearer. I was able to make out most of what they were saying between sobs. They were discussing me, trying to decide what to do. I heard the man talking to Ryer say "I will call her mother." Then I could hear Ryer's conversation. His voice seemed so very far away, yet it was close enough to hear his begging clearly. He was pleading with a man somewhere in the distance not to call our mother, explaining that I would be fine. Sometimes I just got scared. I listened as Ryer clarified to him that it was just a panic attack and all I needed was a little time to calm down before going back home.

The voice talking to Ryer was not coming from the man holding me. He was farther away, and by the sound of his speech, he was rather irritated by our presences. With a bellow, he told Ryer that he didn't care and that we needed to leave. The sense that he didn't want to get involved was obvious in his demeanor. Ignoring the conversation that continued between Ryer and the upset man in the corner, I concentrated on the arms that held me. I was being cradled in sturdy, strong arms, similar to those of my fathers. They were gentle and caring arms similar to my father's in size and strength, but definitely not his. They were the arms of someone who had never held a child close before. Arms that had never been wrapped around a small child's frame closely, hugging and consoling the hurt and sadness away. They were distant, withholding. More like the arms of someone who was unsure of his strength. As if enveloping me within his embrace would somehow hurt me. They were like those of a first time father holding his newborn babe, uncertain of what to do. He was not a man experienced in the art of being a dad, like my own. He was careful and cautious. That was the only way to describe the arms that held me. He was a cautious and careful man, unsure of what to do.

Confused and unable to completely understand what was happening to me, I listened for a voice that I would know. Ryer was here, somewhere close by. I just needed to open my eyes to find him. Listening intently, I heard when the man spoke to Ryer. They were still far away from where I was being held in the arms of someone I didn't know, discussing what was to become of me.

"Okay! Just sit there and don't move. When she can pull herself together, you go straight home and don't stop till you get there." It was silent again, and I could hear no more. Wanting to know that Ryer was okay, I began to will my eyes open—it wasn't easy; I was completely drained.

My eyelids fluttered slowly; unsure of what they would see when they opened completely. Who was this man holding me ever so gingerly? His strange smell was unfamiliar to me. The scent coming from him was strong, again similar to my dad's, but different; more motor oil and gasoline and less outdoor woodsy, farming.

His arms were strong. I could feel the power in them as he held me, the strength that he used to hold me in place, even if it was awkward and unbalanced.

I looked up and into his face; kind eyes layered with concern stared down at me. Only for a fleeting moment was the concern there, then it was gone, replaced by laughter. His smile was huge and his teeth were the biggest I had ever seen. They were pearly white and sparkling clean, compared to the rest of him. He was covered in motor oil, and the reason that he was holding me so awkwardly was probably due to the fact that he didn't want to ruin my yellow sundress. He spoke, and kindness oozed from his words.

"Well, there you are, baby girl!" he said in a velvety voice.

He was so handsome. I stared into his eyes and thought that they were the most beautiful I had ever seen. They were a light golden brown. I had seen them before, but now they were different, different from the light brown of my mother's. No, they were like the color of Grandma Ruth's—caramel, golden brown, just light enough to almost look like a shade of gold.

"Hello," I said, and he began to laugh.

He was a giant; no wonder I could feel the raw strength in his arms when he held me. Now his laughter was shaking his entire body, and mine along with it. Smiling softly at me with his entire being, he safely set my feet to the ground and held onto my shoulders, making sure that I had my balance, before letting go.

Looking up at him, I began to say thank you when I heard Ryer; he was upset. Using his best big-brother disciplinary voice, he scolded me in front of the other man he had been talking to earlier.

"Dylan, what were you thinking? You are going to get us both in trouble!" I could see he was upset but knew immediately that it wasn't directed at me. It was more for the show and benefit of the man behind him. Ryer knew I couldn't help what had happened, and there was no point in being angry with me. Leaning down, he whispered, "It's okay. Are you all right?"

I nodded my head in agreement, and he smiled. Ryer had seen my panic attacks before, and they had always unnerved him. This was the first time that one of my parents was not around to take control of the situation.

I walked the two steps to where Ryer stood and threw myself into his arms. All I could hear was the drumming coming from inside his chest. His heart was pounding madly, surely from the scare I had just given him. Whispering in my ear, he spoke softly, "It's okay, little sis. It's okay." He held me for a short time before pulling away. Looking up into his eyes, I smiled, knowing instantly that all would be well.

Continuing with his show of discipline for the man he had been speaking with earlier, he stared directly into my eyes and sternly scolded me as much as a big brother was allowed. "Ciqala, Dylan, don't scare me like that again, okay?" "Okay, Ryer, I'll try. Sorry," I said with as much conviction as a seven-year-old girl could. "Best behavior." Taking my pointer finger and crossing my heart, I said, "I promise," hoping and praying that this little episode would not end our summer outings together.

He smiled. "All right; let's get that bike chain, okay?"

"Okay," I replied, a smile curving my lips.

Ryer held my hand, and we walked to the man who had been holding me not but five minutes before.

"Excuse me, mister," Ryer interrupted the man as he was repairing a large chunk of metal on his worktable. It was round and looked like a fan was on the end of it. I was pretty sure that it belonged to the car that was now way up in the air, sitting precariously on the lift inside the garage.

"Hi. I wanted to say thank you for helping me with my sister." Ryer extended his hand "My name is Ryer Black, and this is my sister, Dylan."

"Well, Mr. Black, I am pleased to meet you and your very lovely sister Dylan. Is that right?" I could tell that he wasn't questioning my name, but rather the fact that Ryer had called me his sister.

If you lived on the Rosebud Reservation long enough, you would eventually hear the stories of the Black family and their strange adopted daughter. She was the little girl with the white blonde hair and the emerald green eyes that could see deep into your soul and read your mind. It was a bunch of crap. I was never able to do any such thing. I just saw things differently than others. It wasn't as if I had a crystal ball or anything.

It was obvious that this man had never heard of us, giving us the impression he was new to the rez. The big man with the caramel eyes slowly wiped his hand on an old oil rag and extended his hand, grabbing Ryer's and shaking it firmly.

He looked down at me and smiled again, flashing a pearly white smile. Surrounded by a grease-covered face; he was so handsome. It was right then and there that Mr. Mack Goodman became one of my best friends.

Three

Dylan

Hearing the crunch of the tires on gravel as Ty pulled up and parked in front of the beast with the tow truck, I opened my eyes to the realization that I had dozed off for a short period of time.

I watched as Ty jumped from the truck and ran over to where I lay across the hood of the old Chevy. There was nothing slow about Ty; he was what you called a true go-getter. He was always looking for more to do. He was a hard worker, constantly working at top speed, completing one task after another with no complaint. While most young men his age would be out having a good time, Ty would be working extra shifts and helping out the neighbors on his days off. Nothing could slow him down.

"Hi, Ty." I reached out and gave him a huge hug.

"Hey, yourself. How you been?" he asked, flashing that oh-so-sweet dimpled smile.

It was no wonder all the girls at the local high school were chasing him. The last time I came back, at Christmas, Mack said he was chasing away girls from the station with the threat of putting them to work. Some had even agreed to work if they could work alongside Ty. He was turning out to be quite a handsome young man.

I watched as he walked around the back end of the truck and began to pull the cable from the wench. It screeched and whined from underuse and old age, but eventually the screeching stopped and Ty had enough cable to hook up the beast.

I observed him as he concentrated on the cable and beast, determining which way would work best for hauling the broken-down gas hog.

"What are you now, Ty, seventeen?" I questioned him, knowing all too well that he was just about ready to turn eighteen and very excited about his pending birthday party.

Continuing to watch him work, I waited for his reply, knowing that he was hooking the front of the car onto the tow truck and when finished he would give me the answer I already knew. Lying on the ground, positioning the cable and hook under the beast, he looked up and spoke.

"Now, Dylan, don't tell me that you forgot my birthday?" He shifted his eyes and created the sad puppy dog look he knew I could never resist. "You know I was counting on getting a great big dish of your berries cobbler all to myself!" He smiled and gave me a quick wink.

"You know, you keep batting those hazel eyes and talking to the girls the way you do, you are going to end up in a heap of trouble, mister!" I teased.

Still lying on the ground under the front of the beast, he lifted his head to look up at me and with a slight bit of disappointment and worry in his eyes; he said "No, seriously; you are making the cobbler, right?" He stared motionless, waiting for my answer.

I shook my head and just laughed. "Well, when you put it that way, I guess I sort of have to make the cobbler!" I snatched the hat off his head and yanked it onto my own. "I'm keeping the hat!" I teased before continuing. "You know it wouldn't hurt you to try something different for a change." Knowing that I was probably wasting my breath even before I spoke the words, I pressed on, "Maybe a peach cobbler or even a cheesecake. Add a little variety."

If the look on his face was any indication as to what he thought of my suggestions, then I was right on target. He looked up from under the beast again and gave me a look of displeasure, followed by his all-consuming dimpled grin that just made you want to grab him up and squeeze him. "Nah, I think I'll stick with what I know and like." He ducked under the front of the car again.

Ty was easy to like, with his happy-go-lucky attitude and his adorable good looks, it was no wonder most of the opposite sex fell for him.

Even as a young girl, I had grown fond of Ty in a very short time. During the summer months when I was home from school, we spent a lot of time together at the garage. That was where we became great friends. As time passed it became harder and harder to leave and go back to school in the fall.

He was so cute, a little mischievous and totally all guy. I guess you could say with his long black hair and beautiful hazel eyes that most females considered him handsome, but he was like a brother to me. Handsome or not, I liked him for who and what he was, my friend and nothing more.

Ty started hanging out at the station over ten years ago; he was just seven years old at the time, similar to my age when I started hanging out there too. Smarter than most kids of seven, Mack took him under his wing and began training him to be a mechanic. I can still remember his skinny little legs dangling from the side of a car engine that he was repairing, with Mack's help, of course. He was a quick learner, picking up how to get things done and making Mack very proud of his progress. He had been part of our little garage family, the only real family I think he had.

Ty's mother lived across the street from the station. Young and unprepared to be a single mom, Ty was left alone quite a bit. It was a common situation on the reservation, but Ty had been lucky. Many children were not as fortunate as he was to have Mack living next door.

Mack had always said that the reason he took pity on Ty was because of me. He thought that it would be good for me to have a friend who was closer to my age instead of "a couple of old codgers" like him and his father, old Mr. Johnson. He could see I enjoyed Ty's company at the station, and it didn't take long before Ty figured out that he enjoyed being there.

In the beginning, he would come over to the station just to look at the cars, staying for only a short while before old Mr. Johnson began yelling at him to get out of the way. Eventually, his visits became more frequent, and so did the duration of time he spent observing Mack work. As his time expanded watching Mack work, so did his knowledge of mechanics, spurring Mack into making Ty his apprentice. Ty was so pleased that he worked his little body ragged that first month.

He had worked so hard that even Mr. Johnson began warming up to him after a while. He would sneak candy into Ty's pockets, and then act surprised when Ty would ask where it had come from.

The old man was crazy, but I think he liked having Ty around. I know I did. It was like having a baby brother; I had always wanted a younger sibling, and now I had Ty. It was perfect, and we were happy.

Ty eventually took over my job. According to Mack, it was going to be hard to replace me. But if anyone could get the job done, it would be the boy with the hazel eyes and the dimples that just begged to be kissed.

Ty starting working for Mack officially the year I graduated from high school. Supposedly he was replacing my position and taking over for old man Johnson's job as well. I guess old man Johnson was retiring, but if you asked me, he didn't do anything to retire from in the years I worked there.

Everyone knew Mr. Johnson hadn't worked a day since Mack came home, but he stayed on as owner and operator, giving himself a title to claim during the working day. Most days he would just sit on the stoop and play cards with Bill Walters, waiting for something exciting to happen. Not much ever happened in our small town, but if anything did cross those sharp ears, he was sure to give his opinion, whether you wanted it or not.

Mack had taken over the station and turned it around, making some profit for the little shop. Old man Johnson was better off, not that he deserved it by my standards; he was always grumpy and nothing ever seemed good enough for his standards. I always felt he was too hard on Mack, but Mack always took his grumbles and complaints with a grain of salt. I guess it was because he knew that deep down inside, below the hard crusty exterior, old man Johnson was his father and he loved him.

I took to calling him "Saint Mack." He was much stronger and had way more patience for the man than I ever did. I'm sure Mr. Johnson had a heart and all, but I think it was suffering from frostbite. I was just glad Mack was there as well as Ty.

It really didn't matter much to me how Mack ended up on the rez; he was there and I was thankful for it. But according to the story told, old man Johnson had an affair with a mysterious woman, and Mack was the product of that affair.

Being pregnant, young and unmarried, she had wanted to give the baby up. She didn't think she could take care of him. So Mack came to live with Mr. Johnson; only

Mr. Johnson was a single man and had no skills when it came to raising a child, so he shipped him off to his sister's home and rarely saw him. I guess Mack came to visit a couple of times, but never really stayed for very long. Their relationship was a rocky one. It was only years later, when old man Johnson got real sick, that Mack came back and ended up staying to run the garage.

Now Mack runs the shop and Ty works with him, helping out where he's needed. Mrs. T comes in three days a week and keeps his books and the office in order. That used to be my job, along with a few others; when I left for college, Mrs. T took over for me. I guess Ty had a problem keeping the books sorted, so he was banned from the office.

Hearing Ty's movement through my daydreaming, I directed my attention to him and watched as he stepped up his pace to get the beast hooked to the truck. I silently wondered what Mack would do when Ty left.

Mack was the only person I knew who lived and worked by his "schedule" and no one else's. He was never in a hurry to get things done, and he really didn't care if it was screwing up your day or not. He would always say, "My bones only go so fast, and if you want your car fixed right the first time around, then you will have to be patient with me."

Not that Mack was lazy. No, he was a hard worker, and he worked exhausting hours. Basically from sun up till he couldn't stand up any longer. I always wondered why he would push himself so hard, especially for the ranchers who treated him as if he was just some lowly grease monkey. He always told me it wasn't their fault they were so ignorant; they were just born that way.

He was bigger than most men on the rez, and if he wanted to, he could have stood up to them and surely they would have backed down. Yet intimidation was not how Mack dealt with people. He was a gentle giant.

Case in point, a local rancher had come into the shop one day and demanded service right away. Mack walked over, explained he had work scheduled ahead of him and that the ranchers' repairs would get done first thing in the morning. The rancher had argued with Mack for some time. Finally, after seeing he was getting nowhere, he gave up. He did manage to say a few choice words to Mack before he left. I watched as he got in his pickup and angrily sped off down the gravel road.

I questioned Mack as to why he would let anyone talk to him that way. He just shrugged his shoulders and smiled, as if it didn't bother him. It may not have bothered him, but it sure bothered me. I was angry with the rancher, but more so at Mack. Didn't he know he was supposed to stick up for himself? Why would he allow people treat him so badly? My anger at the situation would last for a few hours; I would rant like old man Johnson, fuming at the injustice of it. Then Mack would be Mack and say something silly that would snap me out of it.

"A bird is going to make a perch out of your lip if you stick it out any farther," he'd say, and then he would smile. He could always get me with his smile.

Ty jumped up from the ground, disrupting my thoughts. "Load up, Dylan. She's all hooked up and ready to go. We'll get the old beast back to the shop and see if she's got any life left in her." His enthusiasm was heart-felt; he knew how much I loved the big blue beast.

I walked around to the passenger's side of the truck and climbed in, waiting for Ty to hop in beside me and drive us back to the station. Grabbing the knob of the radio, I tuned in the only station that you could get on the rez and cranked it.

The ride to Mack's was great; Ty and I sang together song after song. He loved music just about as much as I did. He didn't care if we sang out of tune or if the words weren't right, it was just the feeling of letting go and having fun. I missed that. I missed Ty and Mack, and I missed being home.

Continuing to sing off-key and out of tune to the radio, the miles went by quickly. When I saw the edge of town coming into view, I reached over and turned down the radio just enough so I could hear my surroundings as we drove by.

Not much ever changed on the rez; the same old run-down mill was still teetering to the north, waiting for a strong wind to come and blow it over. Only, it never seemed to come, or if it did it was never strong enough to topple the dilapidated building. It was as if there was an invisible string keeping it in place or an unknown force holding onto it, never allowing it to fall.

We crested the next rise, and I could see the two rows of old housing just west of town. They had been built many years ago. The government had built them in an attempt to please the residents and tribal council on the rez, but the contractor had done a horrible job and it wasn't long before they were condemned. Mom said that's what happens when you hire the lowest bidder for the job.

Seeing the condemned housing stirred an old memory of the day Willy Thunder Sky went running home to his mom with a bloody nose. I had hauled off and punched him right in the face for trying to kiss me behind one of those decaying old houses. I had always liked Willy, but he had it coming for not asking my permission. A couple of years later, I made up for it when he did ask permission and I accepted, receiving my very first kiss from him.

It was strange how all the old memories were flying back to me now. I had been home several times since leaving for college in Brookings. Somehow it was different this time, as if deep down inside I knew that this could be my last time I would visit my hometown.

My mind was absorbing every small detail, every visual picture, and every slight memory that came to me, cataloging all of them so that I wouldn't forget.

Continuing to scan the countryside, I recognized several of the small homes that dotted the landscape. There weren't many homes outside of town, unless you were a rancher. The people on the rez seemed to stick close to each other and reside within the town itself.

My hometown of Mission was in complete view now; I could see the small square shape it formed with the seven or eight roads intertwining in a grid fashion. The school was the largest building, taking up a good portion of the east side of town with its massive concrete frame. The parking lot and football field was just to the south of it.

I didn't have many good memories of that school. I was considered a "nobody," an "invisible" by most of my class-mates. Willow and Ryer took care to help me through the early years, but then they graduated and I was on my own. Without them there to protect and shield me from the hurtful words and thoughts that came on a weekly basis, I shut down and stopped trying to make people like me.

Mentally shaking my head at the unsavory memories, I willed them to go away. Only good memories would be accepted on this quick little journey back in time.

With Main Street coming in to view, I scanned to see the few surviving storefronts still intact, all in a neat row lining the worn asphalt of Mission's main drag. As we approached, I could see Minnie's Hair Salon, which was now owned by Willow's best friend, Snow. The old post office next door sat unused after the last postmaster retired and the route became outsourced to the postmas-ter in the next town. Now all the mail came by carrier from either White River or Wood—I couldn't remember which.

As we continued driving down Main Street, we passed several familiar faces, some I had grown up with and oth-ers that I had become acquainted with working at the station. There was nobody of terrible importance that I felt it necessary to stop the truck and say hello to. The town was full with people, not that I should be surprised, it was a beautiful summer day, after all.

It wasn't unusual to see an influx of population on the rez during the summer months. Migrant workers would stay with family members and move to where the work was from month to month. With the job market being non-existent here, most traveled to the larger cities off the reservation for work. Anyone who didn't have to support a family typically traveled with the workers. Anyone who did have a family but couldn't find work usually lived with family members who would support them. Yes, life was very different here on the reservation. It was nothing to see several families living in one home, taking care of each other.

Life was different on the reservation, different than the way people lived in the big cities—or even in the smaller towns, for that matter. On the reservation, everything moved at its own pace, never hurried or rushed. Off the reservation, it was just the opposite: time was money and money was time. Work was top priority off the reservation; once on the rez, it was all about family.

As we turned onto Elm Street and headed for the station, the landscape changed. To the north of town was the open countryside; it was stunning—a painter's dream, really. The beautiful prairie grasslands, with wildflowers speckling the ground and the tall grass swaying in the breeze—it was breathtaking.

When I was a small child and before the bad visions came, my family and I would have picnics in the wide-open spaces of the prairie. I remember them fondly—

running and jumping, chasing each other while playing silly games. Then finally after exhausting ourselves with giggles and laughter, we would sit on one of the many tattered blankets Mom would bring along for us to eat our afternoon meal on. We enjoyed the food she had brought, while taking in the beauty of the reservation. Its prairies and grasslands were a palette of color, from several shades of gold, to rich reds, browns and greens. It was mesmerizing. Eventually, tired from our play and with our bellies full, we would lie in the tall grass and let the rays from the sun warm our bodies, relaxed and completely at peace with Mother Earth. I always loved that feeling.

The ride was almost over as I saw the sign for Mack's place just up ahead. It was a small station with just two stalls for repairs and a tiny office to one side of the building. The junkyard stretched out the back, full of old junkers or "treasures," as Mack called them. It was the only working station for miles, so Mack stayed in business with fuel sales and the minor repairs he did for folks around here. Nothing fancy; Mack didn't need fancy, just functional.

I smiled as we pulled into the yard and watched as Mack came out to greet me. He looked the same, covered in grease and as handsome as ever. Time had been good to Mack; he was moving up there in years, but he still looked strong and vibrant.

Grabbing the handle of the truck, I jerked up hard, releasing the door, and jumped from my seat.

Ty shouted after me as I hit the ground running, "You could have waited until I stopped, before bailing!" I didn't respond; I just kept running until Mack had a firm grip on me and was pulling me into his chest for a huge hug.

"Mack," I shouted, "I've missed you!" I could feel the tears welling up in my eyes as I spoke the words. What was wrong with me? This wasn't as if it was the first time I had been away, and it wasn't going to be last time I would be back. Or was it? I was so unsure of myself. Why was I feeling this way?

Mack squeezed a little harder while kissing the top of my head. "I've missed you too, baby girl."

Leaning back, I looked up at him and smiled. "Okay, when are you going to stop calling me baby girl?" I scolded him meekly. "I am twenty-three now, not really a baby girl anymore." I teased him, knowing that he would never stop calling me his baby girl.

I asked him once why he insisted on calling me the childish nickname instead of my given name, Dylan. He just looked at me and smiled. "The first day that we met, I held you in my arms. You were so tiny and perfect. Fragile, just like a newborn baby. I started calling you baby girl then because to me, you were just that, a baby in a little girl's body. So you will never be anything other than my baby girl," he explained. I never questioned him again, only teased him, so that I could remember.

Mack is a sweetheart of a man and a great mechanic too, but never quite father material, or so he thought. I, of course, had a different opinion. He was the first person besides my family to ever see the "real me," not the person I would pretend to be for the kids and teachers at school. I couldn't be myself around them; if I tried, someone would end up being scared, and I would be sent home for unsavory behavior.

The teachers at the school said I was prone to creating problems or issues. They said I was becoming a bad influence on the children trying to get a good education.

When I was around Mack, my behavior was no different and the issues never seemed to be a problem. Besides my siblings, Willow and Ryer, and parents, Meda and Ezra, Mack was my whole family.

He always had the answers to the tough questions and the uncanny ability to be there when I needed him, almost as if he could hear my thoughts, like the pictures in people's heads I could see before I started pushing them down and hiding them away.

My mom was always there for me too, answering questions, being supportive and doing what she could. My dad, who I know loved me unconditionally, never knew the words to say. Not that he didn't try; it was just too difficult for him to get them out. With Mack, the words would just flow. Mind you, they were few and far between, but they were precise and made a huge impact.

I can remember back when I first got the beast. My father had purchased it for me when I was old enough to drive. He explained the basics and then turned me over to Ryer for my first driving lesson. We drove it slowly to Mack's, first thing. Mack, of course, had to give it the once over. Then he proceeded to inform me of all the responsibilities I now had as a car owner.

My dad never mentioned the big responsibilities such as changing the oil and checking the tire pressure or learning how to take off a flat tire and putting on the spare. I think my dad thought that he would be the one with those responsibilities, but Mack saw it differently.

"It's difficult to find a decent car on the rez, let alone one that will not give up on you and die," he said in a very stern voice. "Making sure that the oil is changed regularly and that the tires are in good shape is important," he stressed as he walked around the four-door metallic blue Chevy Impala. "Your basic upkeep and care of your car will keep it running, long after most other cars die. Take care of her, baby girl, and she will take you far," he had said.

According to Mack, most people don't know how to change the oil in their cars. "It's a crying shame the way folks treat their cars now days," he went on. By the time Mack was done, we had gone through the basics of car upkeep 101 and had scheduled a time for education on oil changes and tire maintenance. I had no idea having a car could be so exhausting.

Mack stepped from our embrace and walked over to where Ty was unhooking the beast. "What happened? Did she give you any warning signs before she quit?" he asked as he walked to the front of the beast.

Reaching under the hood, he grabbed the lever to release it and gently lifted it into place. Once the bar was in position to hold the hood up, he leaned against the front of the engine and began the process of figuring out what went wrong.

"Well, nothing that's not normal for the beast," I replied.

"Did you run out of gas?" Ty said with a sly smirk crossing his face. He would never let me forget the one time I had forgotten to put gas in the beast and she ran dry. It really wasn't my fault, as the fuel gauge had just broken and I could have sworn I had enough fuel to make it home. It was rather embarrassing, and Ty was never going to let me forget it.

"No, smarty pants, I didn't run out of fuel!" I gave him a disgusted look before throwing a grease rag at him that Mack had in his back pocket.

"Now, Ty, leave her alone; can't you see she is upset about the beast?"

I could tell Mack was just ribbing Ty; he thought the fact that I ran the beast dry was funny too, only he would never say so. He just scolded me for being so irresponsible and not paying attention to the basics, and then he threatened to go though basic training on car maintenance with me one more time. I quickly learned my lesson.

"Ha, ha, very funny!" I mocked. "Seriously, Mack, what do you think? Is she fixable?"

"I'm sorry, baby girl, I don't know. Not without digging in and seeing what the problem is." With not much concern in his eyes, he stood up from the engine and looked at me before saying, "I'll take a good look first thing in the morning. I should be able to let you know something one way or the other tomorrow afternoon."

He placed a weathered hand on my shoulder and turned me toward home.

"You go home and give your mother my best; she is probably worried about you and wondering why you haven't arrived yet." With a gentle nudge, he pushed me in the direction of home.

I reached up, gave him a quick hug, and said, "All right, but you are going to have answers for me tomorrow afternoon, right?"

"I'll do my best." He smiled. "Now start walking."

I turned and left the station. I didn't get far before Ty ran up behind me and grabbed hold of my waist and swung me off my feet. Startled, I screamed with surprise.

"Hey, no good-bye for your best friend?" Ty asked.

"Sorry, Ty. Thanks for the tow. You're the best!" I smiled and started heading back toward home. "I'll see you tomorrow afternoon, and we will go to the Badlands after you get off work, okay?"

"Sure thing; see ya tomorrow, Dyl."

"Till tomorrow, then."

Four

Dylan

Following the shortcut path that led from the station to my house, I sauntered home. Ryer and I had made the path when we first started going to the station. We were supposed to follow the street, but it was much faster to cut through the open lots and backyards than to follow the road. We traveled it to the station so often that a path was worn into the ground, becoming a permanent fixture between our house and the shop.

It hadn't been used for a while, so the grass had come back; but there was still the faint impression left in the ground that would only disappear with disuse and time.

I followed it slowly, remembering all the races Ryer and I had to the station on this very path. My eyes wandered, taking in the surroundings. Everything looked the same—the path leading home, the barbed wire fence behind Mrs. T's yard (it was supposed to keep the antelope from eating her garden), and even the tiny red shed sitting behind her back porch. The paint had faded and chipped, but it didn't look much different than the last time I walked the path several months earlier.

I quickened my stride, noticing that the sky was getting a little darker and the sounds of the evening were upon me.

Somewhere in town I could hear a mother hollering for her children to come inside. The scent of food cooking on a stove, and the noticeable lack of traffic walking or driving the streets of Mission was a sure sign the day had come to an end. I was surrounded by the distinct sounds of people settling in for the night.

Farther in the distance you could hear the animals talking; nature speaking to each other, as only they knew how. I always enjoyed listening to them talk. I understood what it was they were saying to each other. Not that I spoke antelope, rabbit, fox, or any other species for that matter; it was more that I could feel the language and see what they were saying inside my head.

I reached the back yard of my childhood home and sprinted the rest of the way to the back door. I was anxious to see my mom, Meda. I missed her terribly. It was difficult when I left for college, not just for me, but for her also. I was her last child to graduate high school and move on to college. Eventually I would be leaving home for good, and that was not something she was looking forward to. She said time and time again, "Oh Dylan, what am I going to do with my time when you've gone too?"

Fortunately, Willow had moved home and married Jackson Talbot. They built a home just west of the school and started their family. Wynn was born in the fall, and she was the most beautiful baby girl I had ever seen. Willow worked at the school as the special education teacher, and Meda babysat young Wynn while her mother was at work.

Ezra was also at home more often. Jackson was working with him on the ranch and taking on a huge part of the workload, allowing Ezra to spend a little more time at home with Meda and his granddaughter.

I reached the backdoor and yanked it open. "Hello, I'm home!" I waited for a response and heard Mom shout, "In here." I followed the sound of my mother's laughter; it was coming from the living room. I rounded the corner to the living room, and there was another giggle and then a squeal of excitement.

"Dilly!" Wynn exclaimed as she toppled over on her not-so-sturdy legs. She had just started running and was still a little wobbly. I swept her up in my arms and blew kisses on her neck. Her giggles were infectious, and I laughed along with her. Placing her back on her feet, slowly I moved back, extending my arms for her to wobble into.

"Now slow down, get your balance." I watched as she took off as quickly as her chubby little legs would carry her, racing to where her mother sat in an armchair on the opposite side of the room.

Willow scooped her daughter up with loving arms and kissed her face all over, before letting go and watching the unsteady little toddler wobble her way to the cat, who was lying peacefully in the corner.

"Hey, Mom." I walked to where my mother sat on the sofa; she was smiling at her granddaughter, who was now busy torturing the cat. I sat beside her and gave her a warm hug.

"Where have you been? I was expecting you here over two hours ago."

"Sorry about that. The beast broke down, and I got held up at the station," I replied.

"It's okay, sweetheart, but you are going to have to go over to Mrs. T's house in the morning and thank her for the beautiful graduation gift that she left for you on your bed," she half-heartedly scolded me.

"No problem, I'll go see her first thing in the morning." I leaned over and planted a huge kiss on her cheek.

Jumping up, I walked to where Willow was now wrestling the screeching cat's tail from young Wynn's hands and mouth. Helping the only way I knew how, I grabbed the slobbering toddler by surprise and threw her up in my arms. Squealing, she let go of the cat's tail but not before taking a healthy bunch of hair with her.

"Oh, Dylan!" Willow scolded. "Please, go wash the hair from her mouth."

"Hi to you too, Willow." I laughed at her anger and carried my bundle to the closest sink. After a good scrub and rinse, Wynn and I walked back into the living room together. Willow gave me the look of disapproval and shook her head. "Mom, I need to get home. Jackson will be there shortly, and I need to get dinner started."

"Okay, sweetheart." I watched as my family exchanged good-byes.

"Good night, little Wynn; Nana loves you." My mother hugged the tiny, wet toddler and handed her to her mother. Willow leaned in for an embrace, "Good night, Willow."

"Good night, Mom. We will see you in the morning." Willow turned to me, and I quickly covered the distance between us. "Good night, Dylan," Willow said.

"Good night, Willow." I reached for Wynn's hand and placed it to my mouth, blowing a quick zurbert onto her freshly washed hands. "Good night, precious Wynn. Auntie Dylan loves you too!"

Willow turned and grabbed the diaper bag that was sitting next to the front door and said a final good-bye. I could hear her talking to Wynn as they walked down the path to her car.

From the front door I watched as she loaded Wynn into the car seat, closed the door, and walked around to the driver's side to get in and go home. She waved a final good-bye to me and drove away.

It was always difficult for Willow and I to get along; I wasn't sure why, but we struggled. Trying to carry a conversation along, without one of us getting upset in the end, was difficult to do. We never saw things the same way; if I said the sky was blue, Willow would say it was green. Even if she knew I was right, she would never admit it.

It wasn't like that with Ryer; our relationship was one of trust and friendship. He never allowed anyone to pick on me, and that included his twin sister. I always wondered if that was the reason Willow and I didn't get along. Did she think I had stolen her twin from her? It couldn't be; Ryer and Willow had been close for some time, until the formidable teenage years, and then they slowly grew apart.

Willow started noticing boys, maturing much faster than Ryer, until he no longer wanted to hang out with her. I then became the tag along with Ryer and his buddies, and I can't remember it ever being any different. I knew that Willow loved me. It may not have been obvious, but she did love me.

At school when the kids were bullying me, she would confront them and strongly suggest they leave me alone. She thought I didn't know or that I wasn't paying attention, but it didn't really make any difference to me. When I tried to thank her, she would blow me off and say I was being stupid. Over and over I would try, but she would only deny helping. Eventually, I gave up.

Closing the front door, I turned to speak with Mom. It had been a long day with little Wynn, and she was tired. I watched as she yawned and started to get up. "Sit, Mom. What do you need? I'll get it."

"I need to get dinner started." She attempted to get up again, and I gently pushed her back down.

I grabbed a lace doily off the back of the couch and placed it over my arm, pretending to be a fancy waiter. "I will take care of it. What would you like to have, madam?"

"Oh, sweetheart, at this point anything you make will be great." She sighed and gave me a smile.

"No problem, grilled cheese and tomato soup it is," I said, then smiled and leaned over to kiss her soft cheek.

Turning around, I walked into the kitchen. I could hear Mom following me. I'm sure she just wanted to make sure I wouldn't burn Dad's dinner.

Grabbing the essentials from the fridge, I walked to the pantry for a can of tomato soup. I made quick work of the lid. I loved the new pop-off tops; no more can openers. Dumping the contents of the can into a pot and then adding the correct amount of milk, dinner was started. Slowly I stirred the soup and watched as the heat radiated from the stove.

Mom approached as I was stirring and reached for the spoon. I relinquished it to her and moved to the counter to make the grilled cheese.

"I'm home!" I listened as my father hung his work coat up on the hook at the back door and removed his boots.

"We're in here," Mom hollered back. His approach was slow; my father was getting older, and he had worked hard all of his life. You could hear the ache in his walk as he moved though the house and into the kitchen.

"Hello, beautiful." He wrapped his arms around my mother and kissed her neck. They swayed in each other arms, a ritual that never grew old seeing.

"Mmmm, something smells good. Whatcha cooking?"

"Your daughter is making you grilled cheese and tomato soup."

"Well now, that sounds delicious." He stepped behind me to give a quick squeeze and a peck on my cheek.

"Hey, Dad, would you like me to make some sausage to go with this?" I asked.

"Sure, that would be nice. I could use a little extra tonight." He squeezed me again and walked to the bedroom hallway. "I'll jump in the shower and be right out."

"Okay, Dad. Dinner will be ready when you're done."

Dinner went by quickly. I cleared the table and did the dishes. After a few quick kisses, hugs and good nights, I was off to bed.

Entering my room, I noticed a very large package sitting on the bed. It must have been the gift Mrs. T left for me. Picking it up, I began to unwrap it. The paper was beautiful. It was homemade out of light brown paper and stenciled with green ivy, and dotted with delicate flowers. A large lavender bow accented the center.

It was lovely and so like Mrs. T. She had the uncanny ability to make something out of what most would see as nothing. I was pretty sure that I knew what was inside the beautiful wrapping. A quilt. Mrs. T made one for all of us kids when we graduated from college. After all, it wasn't often that a small-town kid from Mission, South Dakota, made it though all four years. Most only lasted a year or so before they got homesick and yearned for the reservation.

The Black children were different. Each of us had gone to college and graduated. Ryer was an engineer in Sioux Falls. He had a great job working for the electric company. Willow, of course, was a special education teacher, working right here in town.

As for me, well, I had yet to determine what it was that I would be. I had a degree in business, but I didn't know exactly what it was that I wanted to do. In fact, I had changed my major so many times that I was confusing my student counselor and quickly becoming a pain in his side. The truth was, I loved school. If I could have afforded the tuition, I would still be enrolled today.

I finished opening the packaging and pulled out the most stunning quilt I had ever seen. Mrs. T had outdone herself. It was beautiful; a collage of wildflowers in greens, golds, deep reds, and rich browns. It was as if she captured the grasslands on fabric and had sewn them all together.

Caressing the quilt, I could feel the detail she had put into every block. It was perfect, and I loved it. I would make sure I thanked her properly, maybe running a few errands or possibly helping her with her garden. Tomorrow would be good; it could wait until then. I would think about it some more and figure out exactly what to do. Right now, I was exhausted. I could barely keep my eyes open.

Quickly changing into my pj's, I crawled into bed. Stretching out like a cat against the cool sheets of the bed, I relaxed. In a matter of moments, I was asleep.

"No, no, stop! You can't!" I screamed myself awake.

Shaking, sweat pouring off my body, I stared at the covers wrapped around my legs in a strangle hold. Every muscle in my body was tense. Grabbing at the blankets and coverings, I untangled them from my limbs and slowly slid to the edge of the bed.

Letting out a long held breath, I shivered as the air I released from my lungs came out in puffs around my face. Slumping my shoulders forward, I instinctively knew. He was back, but why?

Five

Dylan

"Good morning, Mrs. T." I smiled as she opened her front door.

"Dylan, sweetheart; come in, come in," she replied while motioning to enter with her hands.

Mrs. Emily Thundercloud had been our neighbor for as long as I can remember. She was a widow with no real family. There was a cousin who came to visit once in a rare while. On one of those rare visits, I had seen him. He was not what you would call the typical Native American. He had long blonde hair, very similar to my own, and the same delicate features that I carried. I asked Mrs. T about him, and she just said that he was a distant relative on her husband's side of the family.

"How are you, Dylan? Are you home for a long visit?" Mrs. T asked.

"I'm great, thanks." I followed as she walked through the tiny front room and into the kitchen. "No, it won't be a long stay; I will be leaving as soon as I get the beast up and running."

"Really? I got the impression from your mother that you would be here for a while."

"Yeah, about that…I haven't had the heart to tell them, but I got a job in Rapid City. I start in a couple of weeks."

"I see. You should really tell your mother soon. I think she has already started making plans for your summer."

"I know, and I will. I just have to find the right time."

It was never easy speaking with my parents about leaving the reservation. They were always so concerned about my welfare. It was hard enough getting them to let go when I left for college. Moving to Rapid for work was a topic that I knew would not go over well.

"So what brings you to my little house?" Mrs. T asked.

I watched as she stood over the sink, scrubbing the dirt off some potatoes. Mrs. T had the best garden in Mission; she planted everything from baby carrots to summer squash and green bell peppers. They all flourished under her watchful eye.

"I just wanted to stop by and say thank you for the quilt, it is perfect. I love it." Leaning in, I gave her a quick hug.

"You're welcome, dear. What did you think of the pattern?"

I knew exactly what she meant. Normally she would have made a star quilt; she had made one for both Willow and Ryer, but mine was different. She knew I would appreciate the beauty of nature that was designed within the quilt itself.

"It's lovely, and I will cherish it always!" I watched as she finished her chore and moved to dry her hands on the towel next to the sink.

"Well, I am glad you like it. I knew if anyone would appreciate the life and beauty it represented, it would be you." She tossed the towel down and walked the two steps to the back door, swinging it open she waved for me to follow.

"I'm glad you stopped. Come, I want to show you something."

I followed her out the door and down the three steps into her backyard. We walked to the end of the faded little red shed and turned the corner. I knew instantly what she was taking me to see. The rosebush I had planted with her so many years ago had finally grown large enough that it was blooming.

"Oh my gosh, Mrs. T! It's finally blooming!"

"I thought you would be happy to see its first roses." she smiled. "Notice the color."

I did notice. The blooms were a lovely shade of pale yellow, similar to the look of creamy butter. It had been over four years since we had planted the rose bush. It had begun growing and then just stopped.

Mrs. T and I had labored over it and waited for the blooms to come. I had finally given up last year when I convinced myself they would surely show themselves and then preceded not to. I had really high hopes for it at one time, and I wasn't sure why. After all, I had gotten the bush on a fluke.

A gentleman passing through town had stopped at the station to fill up his car before getting back on the road. He had cleaned out his back seat and found the little pot containing the neglected rosebush. He said he had bought it for his wife and forgot to give it to her. He was about to throw it away, when I asked if I could have it. Happily he placed it in my hands.

It was in rough shape, and looked as if it hadn't seen water in several days. I carefully set the tiny bush on my desk in the station office and gave it a small amount of water. Not wanting the little plant to go into shock from overwatering, I coaxed a little life back into it throughout the rest of my workday.

Walking home with my new treasure, I stopped at Mrs. T's to see if she would begin work on Monday at the station. I would be leaving soon for college and needed to show her the ropes.

She saw the fragile plant in my hands and asked what I planned to do with it. It was then that we decided to plant the sickly little bush on the side of her house, next to the faded red shed.

I left for college shortly afterwards, and every summer when I returned, I would check to see if the little bush had made it through the winter. Every summer it would be the same. Still alive, a little bit of growth, but no roses anywhere in sight.

"I wondered what color the blooms would be." Leaning down, I sniffed the fragrant bud.

"Well, that little bush was in tough shape when we planted it here." She smiled. "It took the last four years to show its true colors."

I looked up from my bent position and smiled, knowing full well that there was a lesson in the words she stated. I could tell just from the way she spoke that she had something to say or wanted something that only I could give. I stood from my crouched position. With hands on hips, I asked, "Okay, Mrs. T, what's up?"

"Nothing. Why does something have to be up?" Shrugging her shoulders, she smiled. "I was just thinking that since you're only going to be here for a short time that you could help with the garden before leaving town." She smiled and began walking to the garden in question.

I was born with a green thumb, and Mrs. T knew it. I had the uncanny ability to bring the best out in plant life. With the exception of the little rose bush, I could get a garden to grow almost anywhere and there were several gardeners in Mission who were envious of that fact. The little rose bush was the only plant that gave me a difficult time. Mrs. T thought that it was because I wasn't around enough to give it the love it needed.

"Well, is that all? I suppose I could chip in and give this weed-infested patch of soil some attention and turn it into a garden."

I could see the grimace on her face at my description of her small garden, which was the farthest from the truth it could be. Mrs. T had a green thumb too; in fact, it was her talent for gardening that peaked my interest to begin with.

"Now, listen here, young lady! Not everyone has your talents!" she scolded.

"Calm down, Mrs. T. I was only joking," I teased. "I would love to work in your garden. It's the least I can do to show my thanks for the quilt." Smiling at her, I knew I was forgiven for my insensitive remark.

"Well, good. It's hard on my old bones, all that getting up and down from the ground." She went on, listing her complaints as she turned and went back inside. I could just make out the final words about pulling weeds and too much work before she closed the screen door and was gone. I laughed and shook my head at her comment about old bones; she wasn't much older than my mother.

Now alone, which was better, I could concentrate on what I was doing without interruption. I studied the layout of the small garden and could tell that Mrs. T had not deviated from the original design we had made together many years ago. Everything was where it needed to be and it looked as if Mrs. T had planted on time. The small plants were just having a difficult time surviving due to a lack of care, probably because Mrs. T was working more, both at the station and the school as a teacher assistant. The abundance of weeds that were choking out the plants would have to go and with a little more water, all would be well.

Grabbing a rubber band from my jeans pocket, I pulled my long blonde hair into a ponytail and got to work. I made short work of the weeds. After pulling continuously for an hour, the final nuisance was plucked from the soil.

I hummed with the sounds of nature, making music with the wind in the trees, the buzzing of bees, the chirping of birds and many others creatures who lived there. I worked at nurturing the small plants back to life. Slowly I turned the soil around each plant, speaking to it as if it were a child.

I had just finished watering the last row of carrots when the breeze changed directions and the voice of someone singing was being carried on the wind. It was beautiful. I could not make out the words, if there were any, but her voice was seductive, almost entrancing, as if she were singing to her lost love. Then I realized that the voice was coming from me.

Startled, I dropped the hose and slapped a hand across my mouth. Dazed and a little bewildered, I observed the garden again. Only this time, it was not the same garden. The tiny plants that I had just labored over for the past couple of hours were huge in comparison.

I didn't understand; only two or three hours ago they were barely surviving and now they were healthy, strong, and producing. The tomato plants had small green orbs drooping from their limbs, waiting to turn ripe. The corn stalks were at least six feet in height and the carrots were bursting from the soil, begging to be pulled.

What had just happened? I knew I was good, but not that good.

Backing away from the garden, I bumped into Mrs. T. She had come to check on my progress. Startled again, I jumped and let out a blood-curdling scream.

"Hey, are you okay?" Mrs. T grabbed my shoulders, holding me an arm's length away.

I stood there, staring at her in shock and gasping for air. Filling my lungs with what was surely my life breath, considering the fact that I had just scared myself half to death and skimmed a couple of years off my young life.

"Yeah, sure. I'm fine. I just scared myself. Guess I am just tired."

"Well, I should think so! You have been out here all morning and most of the afternoon, working on this garden." She turned toward the garden, and I could see a quick flash of disbelief run across her face before she masked it with a smile.

"You've done a wonderful job, Dylan. Now come inside; let me get you a tall glass of iced tea." She smiled at me, and I watched as she leaned over and pulled a carrot from the ground, brushing the dirt from its skin, before biting off the tip.

I couldn't believe it; was she seeing the same garden that I was? She had to notice the complete transformation that had taken place in just a few hours. I waited for her to say something, anything, but she only walked to the back door of the house and grabbing the handle, pulled the door open. "Are you coming?"

I stood there waiting, stuck in time, not knowing what to do next. Finally, as if coming out of a daze, I shook my head and stepped from the garden.

"No, I need to get going. I didn't realize how late it was. Mack is expecting me." The sky was getting darker, and it was approaching late afternoon. I must have worked in the garden a lot longer that I had thought. I turned and began to walk away, when Mrs. T called for me.

"Dylan, thank you for all your help today." Smiling, she said, "The garden looks great."

I smiled back and just nodded in reply. Turning, I headed for the path on the other side the of barbed wire fence.

Six

Dylan

Move faster, that's what I needed my feet to do, was move faster. It seemed that they weren't moving fast enough; even running it felt like I was moving in slow motion. After I had crawled through the fence and was sure that Mrs. T could no longer see me, I sprinted toward the station.

The breeze created by my running felt good. I had gotten hot tending the garden and hadn't noticed it until just now. What had happened back there? I had obviously lost track of time. I thought I had only been working for a couple of hours, when in actuality it had been all morning and most of the afternoon.

I was so confused. Had I just misjudged Mrs. T's garden, or had it looked like that the whole time? Maybe I just couldn't see the plants well with all the weeds crowding them. That had to be it. I continued running and by the time I got to the station I had convinced myself that the garden had been just fine and once I pulled the weeds away, you could see its beauty.

I slowed my pace as I turned the corner and walked the rest of the way to Mack's station. I could see the beast sitting to the side of the lot, looking pathetic and used up. I had a very good feeling that I was going to get some very bad news, and I wasn't looking forward to it.

Mack was sitting behind the desk as I entered the station office. Nothing much had changed about the office. One desk in the center of the room, with a framed picture of a nineteen sixty-eight Dodge Charger hung beautifully behind it.

Mack was reclining in the abused leather chair with his feet perched on the corner of the desk. To the left of him, a couple of filing cabinets sat in the corner. I grabbed one of two black stools that sat in front of the desk for customers to use and sat down.

"Hey, so what's the verdict?" I questioned Mack.

"Hello, Mack! How are you, Mack?" he teased, raising a disapproving eyebrow before continuing on. "No! Just straight to the thick of it." he teased again.

"Sorry. Hi, Mack." Smiling, I gave him the look that always won him over.

"That's better." He stood up from the chair and walked around the desk. "Where have ya been? I was expectin' to see you some time ago."

"I was helping Mrs. T with her garden and lost track of time."

"I see. Did you help her get it fixed up? She was complaining about the fact she never seemed to have time to work in the garden because she was always here or at the school, busy with work."

Still feeling a little strange about what had just happened, I nodded my head nonchalantly and stood up from the stool.

"Yeah, it looks great. So, about the beast..."

Mack walked out of the office and proceeded to where the beast sat, waiting for my return. I followed and said a silent prayer that she would be fixable just one more time.

"I'm sorry, baby girl, but the beast has seen her final days. It would cost more for the parts to fix her than she's worth."

"What? How can you say that? You can't put money on love." Shaking my head, I leaned over and lay on the hood of the beast dramatically, "She's my baby, Mack; can't you *please* save her?"

"Oh, Dylan! Stop with the drama. It may have worked on me when you were younger, but it is a little silly now." Mack shook his head and continued, "The beast needs to be retired. However, I may have a solution to your transportation problem."

Quickly I stood up to give him my full attention. "What? Do you have a car that you have been working on?"

"Nope, even better," Mack said.

The smile that covered Mack's face was huge; I could feel the excitement bubbling up inside of me and couldn't wait for what he was about to say. My imagination ran away with me. What could be better than a working car, one that he had fixed up? Following Mack, we went inside the station and walked to the first stall.

A beautiful Ford F150 pickup was sitting there, calling my name. The excitement that had begun to bubble up inside of me was now overflowing. I could feel my body jumping with joy and the smile that spanned my face was so big, it felt as if my skin would crack from the pressure.

"No way! Oh my God, no way!" Walking around to the front of the truck, I let my hand glide over the glossy exterior; then racing to the driver's side, I yanked open the door and jumped inside the cab.

Beautiful! That the only way to describe what I was seeing. The beast had never been beautiful; functional, yes, but beautiful it was not.

I had a whole lot of wonderful memories of the beast, but this was beyond compare. Staring at the dash, I absorbed every detail, each dial, button and switch, from the radio to the windshield wipers. I was so engrossed with my investigation of the air conditioning, that I didn't notice Mack holding an old green bicycle, dotted with rust spots, until he tapped on the window.

Sliding from the plush interior of the pickup, I repeated my words again, but this time with disappointment and a little bit of anger. "No way! Oh my God, no way!"

Mack just laughed and shook his head. "Did you really think that I got you a forty-thousand dollar pickup to replace the beast? That thing costs more than my house!" he laughed.

"Not funny, Mack!" I scolded. "You should have stopped me right away instead of letting my imagination get the better of me!"

"What, and miss the look on your face when you saw the green machine?" His laughter increased.

"You just wait! I'll get you back for that little stunt!" I huffed.

"Oh, come on. You have to admit, the look on your face was priceless. Woohoo; good stuff that was!" He nudged me with his elbow and smiled before saying what I already knew.

"Baby girl, that pickup you are in love with, well, it has a price tag. And baby girl, you can't afford it." He pushed the bike forward for me to grasp. Looking at Mack with his matter-of-fact, no-nonsense, this-is-how-it-is attitude, I conceded.

I had no business thinking that a truck like that could be mine. Mack would never have spent a small fortune on a vehicle when the majority of the people in Mission could barely afford the necessities in life.

I took the green machine, as he affectionately called it, from him and gave it the once over.

"All right, I know you're right. It was just nice to think that maybe…" Looking to the bike again, "Thanks for the green machine; I will ride it every day" I stated sarcastically.

"You're welcome, baby girl. Ya know it's only temporary; Ty and I are going to look for a fixer-upper in Rapid."

I watched as he bent over to check the back tire of the green machine before continuing. "Ty told me about your plan to leave soon." I could feel my shoulders tensing, but before I could say anything, Mack continued speaking.

"We'll drive you up and help you get settled into your new apartment before you start working at that fancy accounting place." He looked at me with understanding, and I melted.

Tears filled my eyes. "You're the best, Mack." Leaning forward, I wrapped my arms around his shoulders. With the green machine sandwiched between us, it was difficult to get a good hold. Releasing him, I stepped back and smiled.

"Well, I guess the green machine will have to do." Swinging my leg over the bike, I straddled the worn seat.

"Just take care of her and she should last until we can replace the beast."

"I will. Thanks again, Mack."

Mack continued with his tutelage on bike maintenance. "I greased the chain and changed the tubes in the tires. She's in good shape, but I wouldn't be taking her for any bike tour." He continued, "Make sure to check the chain every day and keep it clean."

I placed my hand on his should gingerly as if to say "I know." He worried about me, and it was very sweet, but I could take care of myself and if he had taught me anything over the years, it was how to maintain a vehicle, even if it was a worn-out old bicycle.

"I am going to be just fine, Mack." I watched as some of the tension rolled from his shoulders and he smiled back at me.

"I know that, but I can still worry, can't I?" he said.

"I don't know why. You have done a great job teaching me, and I am beginning to get the impression that you don't trust me."

"All right, I get it, no more," he conceded.

Sitting down on the worn seat, I wiggled to see how sturdy she was, resting with my foot on one pedal and the other on the ground for balance. I knew that there was more he wanted to say, there always was, and his going on about the bike was just a distraction to keep from asking.

"So, are you going to tell me what's really up, or do I have to guess?" I asked.

"I don't know what you're talking about," Mack replied.

Tilting my head to the side, brows raised, I gave him the whatcha-talking-about look. Grinning, he turned and walked away. Pushing the green machine with me, I followed as he lifted the garage door and walked out of the station stall.

"Come on, Mack. What's eating at you?" I asked.

He turned, looking back at me straddling the bike, and waited for what he had to say.

"Have you told your parents yet, baby girl?" he finally asked.

Knowing all too well what he was referring to, I nudged the bike forward and was going to leave when he grabbed the handlebars to stop me.

Mack had always been supportive in everything I did. When my parents were being overly protective and unwilling to bend, I would turn to Mack. It had gotten him into quite a few confrontations with my father. After the last incident, I swore I would never involve him again. I stared at his grease-cracked hands on the bike handle, holding it in place.

"No," I said.

You could feel the reaction in his body when he heard my answer. He was upset, and I knew I had to say something, and quick. Letting go of the bike, he turned and walked to the station office.

"Mack, what are you doing?" Dropping the kickstand on the bike, I jumped off and quickly followed him.

"I'm calling your parents. They need to know. You promised me you were going to tell them some time ago and you haven't, so I guess you have forced my hand." He moved into the small station office faster than I thought possible and headed for the phone.

"Mack, please! I will tell them. I just haven't found the right time," I pleaded and watched as he picked up the receiver and began to dial.

"You said that before, baby girl; I am not going to have your father coming—"

"Okay, okay, okay. I know you're right. I will go and tell them right now." Desperate, I interrupted him in mid-tirade.

"I just don't want to upset them; you know how they are, always so overprotective."

Mack walked to where I stood feeling rather over-whelmed and a little dejected. Placing his hands on my shoulders and squeezing lightly, he gave me his version of a pep talk. "You would think that a twenty-three-year-old woman would be able to tell her parents she is moving out and has a great job in the city." I could feel the warmth and concern in Mack's arms as he wrapped them around me.

"Now, come on, baby girl, you're the last chick to leave the nest. I'm sure it is difficult for them." Empathy was not an emotion Mack usually felt for my parents. It was strange to hear it coming from him now. I broke the embrace and stepped back.

"Okay, what did they say to you? Did Dad come down on you again … ?" I asked.

"No, it's nothing like that. It's just that Meda stopped in the other day and wanted to know if I had heard from you. I told her not recently, but it seems that you have been rather distant with her and she was concerned." He paused to watch my reaction. "She loves you, baby girl; she's just worried if you ask me, she has every right to be."

Stepping from the tiny office, my mind began running through all of the times Meda had been troubled by my strange behavior, and the stress I had put both my parents through by being different from other children. The countless sleepless nights, the strange happenings that could not be explained; I knew without a doubt that I was different, and as hard as I tried to fit in, I was never what you would call normal.

The visions in my head, which I had successfully held at bay for the most part, locked down deep inside, weren't the only strange happenings they had to deal with. I had uncanny ability with animals, knowing what they were thinking or needing, as if I could speak to them, and the strange sense that I was able to move or control my environment to some degree.

I smiled as I remembered finding a nest of baby skunks snuggled in with their mother for an afternoon nap. I watched as they curled up together and peacefully slept. While watching, I had become tired too, and lay beside the family of skunks, napping until I heard my mother's call. She had been worried and came looking for me.

Ryer was with her, and I could hear the concern in their voices. Waking completely from my slumber, I realized the family of skunks had curled into my body for warmth and were now awake from my stirring. I smiled at the tiny creatures and stroked their coats.

Meda's voice came to me again, and I stood, preparing to walk to her. I had only made it a few feet when I heard the rustling behind me. Ryer appeared in the tall grass. I jumped at his sudden appearance, and so did the mother skunk.

Ryer turned to run, but it was too late; he was completely covered in her spray. It would be days before the smell was gone, and naturally, Meda forbid me to play with the animals again.

Mack's voice broke into my thoughts, "Dylan, did you hear me?"

Shaking the memories from my mind, I questioned, "I'm sorry; what did you say, Mack?"

He approached me slowly and placed his hands on my shoulders. "I said, go home, Dylan. Talk to Meda and Ezra; they love you, and they will understand. You are, after all, a grown woman now. You need to begin your life, off the reservation."

Smiling at him, I knew he was right. It was just going to be hard to convince my parents that I could take care of myself without having to have someone watch over me. Even at college they had me living with family, making sure that I checked in on a regular basis. I had only agreed to live with Uncle Tim and Aunt Phyllis because it would save on expenses, as I needed every dime I had for tuition.

I would have preferred living in the dorms and experiencing college life like the rest of the students enrolled, but as it turned out, not only was I saving money for my classes but my parents had the benefit of a watchful eye in my relatives.

"Okay, I get it. I will go and talk to them tonight. No more stalling, cross my heart." I ran my fingers across my chest and smiled, hoping that Mack was convinced and would not take matters into his own hands.

We walked together back to where the green machine stood propped up by its wobbly kickstand, and I grabbed for the handlebars. Pushing up the kickstand, I began to turn the bike in the direction of home.

Noticing the beautiful truck again, I nodded to her and asked "So, I know she's not mine, and she is *so* totally not yours; so who does this beauty belong to?" I looked to Mack for answers. "Please don't tell me Mr. Hall has bought another new toy for his spoiled brat."

Mr. Hall was a local rancher near Mission. In his younger years he had purchased a lot of land from the locals for little or no money, then turned around and leased out those large acreages to distant ranchers. They were shipping in cattle by the truckloads. He was making a killing, until the rustling began. Trucks would come in the middle of the night and take all the unbranded new head and move them out.

Of course, the ranchers who had leased his land and services sued Mr. Hall. Their claim was that he hadn't protected their investments by allowing this rustling to happen right under his nose. It was quite the scandal; several people speculated he had taken the cattle himself and sold them to pay off his son's gambling debts. Old man Johnson had enjoyed that little tidbit when it crossed his path.

"No, it's not Mr. Hall's truck. I don't think that he can afford a Toyota right now, much less a Ford F150." He smirked, knowing the trouble that Mr. Hall was in.

"No, this beauty belongs to a stranger; can't remember his name off the top of my head. I wrote it down on the paperwork in the office." I listened and watched as Mack walked the length of the truck, admiring the beauty of its exterior.

"I guess he and his nephew are in town visiting a relative; they dropped it off and asked if I'd take a look at it, said the engine was sounding funny." A frown creased his brow and I had to ask.

"So what's wrong with it?" I asked.

"That's just it, baby girl; I can't find anything wrong with her, she sings like a hummingbird," Mack replied.

"Well, I guess they were mistaken. At least you got to look under the hood and play with her a bit." Mack just smiled and continued walking with me to the street.

I pushed the green machine to the road and jumped onto the seat; placing a foot on the pedal, I gave it a strong shove and took off. Glancing back, I could see Mack raise his hand in farewell.

"Good night, Mack; thanks for the green machine. I will see you in the morning."

"Bye, baby girl. Talk to your folks!" he yelled after me. "See ya in the morning."

I continued my ride home in deep thought. How was I going to explain to my parents that I needed some distance from them and the rest of the family without hurting their feelings? I knew they would be upset, not to mention angry at the fact that I had been withholding information from them.

I accepted a job I had applied for over a month ago. Mack had been the only one I had told. I was so excited that I had received the job offer that I wanted to tell someone, so I called Mack. He would be happy for me; I could share my good news with him and not be afraid he would dampen my spirits with unfounded concerns.

I pedaled faster; the night sky was approaching quickly. I could see the faint shape of the crusty moon forming in the sky and knew it would be dark soon.

I was almost home when little Taylor Matheson captured my attention. She was in the front yard of her home, playing with a small pup that couldn't be more than a few months old. The sound of her giggles distracted me from the road, and I didn't see the man in the street until it was too late.

The green machine and I were hurdling toward him. I tried applying the brakes, but they weren't working properly. Mentally I recycled everything Mack had said and cursed myself for not checking them.

As if in slow motion now, I could feel the impact that was coming. I dropped my feet from the pedals and started dragging them, hoping to slow the bike as much as possible. Now only inches from him, I closed my eyes and waited for the inevitable. I felt the wind blow through my hair. Opening my eyes, I could see only the road stretched out in front of me. The bike was slowing down, and I was almost at a complete stop.

I had hit nothing.

Whipping my head around, I scanned the roadside, looking for the man who had been in front of me just moments ago, thinking that he must have jumped out of the way. But he wasn't there.

Now completely stopped and in the middle of the road, I twisted around; straddling the bike, I looked in the general direction of where he had been.

He was still there, in the same exact spot; the same spot where a collision should have taken place. I had expected to see him lying off to the side of the road after jumping out of harm's way, removing his body from the road and the obvious collision. Yet there he stood, unruffled, looking rather fine in a light gray shirt and blue jeans with his shoulder-length hair windblown, and a smile on his face that would surely melt any girl's heart.

I had missed him, but how? I didn't think that I had had enough time to divert the bike completely to avoid him, but somehow I must have managed it.

I watched as he smiled at me and turned to walk away, striding to the side of Mrs. T's house. I yelled after him, "Hey, mister, where are you going?" I watched as he walked around the side of Mrs. T's home and disappeared from my view.

Curious, I pushed the green machine to the side of the road and propped it up, using the kickstand. Walking across Mrs. T's front yard, I headed for the side of the house. The mystery man had disappeared around the corner, and my intentions were to follow him and to apologize. I hadn't gotten far before noticing a strange light coming from inside Mrs. T's home.

Noticing the light, my attention was diverted, and before I was able to locate the mystery man, I found myself moving toward the house.

The light was unusual, in the sense that I had never seen anything like it before. Growing up next door to Mrs. T, I knew her and her home just as well as I knew my own family and home.

Darting another quick glance to the corner of the house where the mystery man had disappeared, I shrugged and completed my changed course.

As I approached the front steps of Mrs. T's home, I began questioning myself. *Do I really want to go inside and see what the light is?* It was late, after all, and Mrs. T would more than likely ask me to stay and visit some more. I had already had enough weirdness for the day, and the light coming from her home only looked to prove to be more of the same.

Stretching forward to get a better glimpse through the front entrance, I convinced myself that I should check on her and make sure she was okay.

Her front door was swung completely open and the screen door was the only barrier keeping me from entering the house. During the summer nights, when the heat of the day was gone, most residents would leave their windows and doors open for the cool night air.

Peering inside, I noticed that the light was coming from the kitchen, just out of direct view for anyone who might be looking in from the street. Slowly I opened the screen door and walked inside. Approaching with some apprehension and unsure why, I crept forward, strangely uncomfortable, yet somehow feeling a sense of familiarity. However, the feeling of familiarity didn't stop the hair on the back of my neck from standing straight up.

It wasn't as if I wasn't welcome in Mrs. T's home; I had walked through that door hundreds of times and announced that I was there. Why was I having so much apprehension now? Somehow this evening was different;

this time something felt wrong, very wrong; but what? Pushing down the uncomfortable feelings that were creeping up my spine, I stepped further into the house.

Grabbing every bit of inner strength I had, I walked toward the small kitchen and the light illuminating within. Calling out to Mrs. T as I did so, "Mrs. T, are you hom…" My words trailed off as I rounded the corner of the kitchen and saw a man sitting across from Mrs. T at the small kitchen table. I had never seen or met him before, but I was positive that I would never forget him.

He was pale in coloring, almost luminous—very exotic and quite handsome. His long, snowy white hair cascaded down his back and looked as if it had recently been slightly windblown. He was dressed in what could only be described as a loose gray tunic, and his brilliant crystal blue eyes were watching me.

Tapping quickly into my senses, I could feel no sense of anger or deception coming from him. It was more like he was happy, pleased that I had walked in. Even with all the familiarity and openness I felt coming from him, it wasn't his presence that captured my full attention.

He was looking at me, waiting for my next move, and I was looking at it. I stared, frozen, dumbfounded at what I was seeing. In the center of the table, floating about a foot above its surface was the source of the light.

An orb: that was the only word that I could use to describe what I was seeing. Maybe a crystal ball; but no, it had no borders, no form of containment, it just floated in a circular motion, translucent, a brilliant golden glow.

There were strands of light, thousands of them, some brighter than others, circling around, floating within the orb. Then there were the pictures—my family's faces were there, first Meda and then Ezra, little pieces of my life, almost like snapshots drifting through the golden strands. I watched the pictures as they floated though one after another.

The first day of kindergarten, my fifth birthday, Christmas at home, they were all there; all the wonderful memories of childhood. I continued to watch as the strands of my life showed everything, good and bad. High school, leaving for college, dating, first crush, breaking up; the pictures were a play-by-play of my life leading up to this day.

I was mesmerized; faster and faster the pictures were floating though the orb. I was barely aware that Mrs. T had moved from the table to stand beside me.

Then the orb began to change; the once brilliant light began to darken and the golden strands were slowly disappearing.

It seemed as if the translucent orb of golden light was being clouded with black smoke, blocking any rays of light that may try to show itself. The happiness that was once there was now gone, replaced by emptiness and a sense of dread.

Pictures began to float through the orb again. I could see my face, and for a brief moment I thought that the orb would show me the light once again.

I was wrong, the pictures were back; but this time it wasn't of the life that I had already lived, but the life that was to be my future.

I saw nothing there but blackness, pain, and despair. The pictures floated on strands of blood red, and they continued one after another with the same shocking results. Pain, pain, and more pain; then he was there.

I watched as the black figure with the dark glowing eyes from my childhood nightmares plunged a dagger into my chest. He stood over my lifeless body and shouted in triumph, like a hunter with its kill. Finally, death consumed me. My life was gone and replaced by nothingness.

I heard the scream come from my mouth. I had just seen my death at the hands of the dark man. I turned my head to Mrs. T, questioning, "What's happening?" Who was the man sitting at her table? I needed answers. Before I could ask them, I felt my body sway, and then the air was gone from my lungs, and I was falling.

Seven

Alessar Belmonte

"Gelmir, are you ready? We need to get going." Leaning through the open doorway, waiting for a response and sharpening my senses, I listened and heard nothing. Venturing forward slowly, I stepped into the tiny dwelling Gelmir called his home.

Gelmir, unknown to me at the time, had come into my office representing himself as a person of interest. My first impression of him was one of complete and utter control. He was a man who seldom ever showed emotion and could bend others easily to his will.

Strangely distinguished looking, he carried himself with a surety that most men would find intimidating.

Not that his stature was one of mass or strength; no, he was not a large man, but rather average in size. His long, wheat-colored hair was worn pulled back with a leather tie, allowing the features of his face to be seen more clearly.

He had a handsome face, one that had seen many years. Time had not ravaged his delicate features, but rather had given him a look of nobleness. Yet, it was the brilliance of his blue eyes that captured attention; they were eyes of a man who had seen much in his lifetime and carried secrets, many secrets.

Dressed in long robes that looked to be decades old and carrying a book that had seen several centuries by the look of its binding, he revealed his motive for being in my office.

He claimed he knew who I was and if I wanted the answers to the questions that had been plaguing me for centuries; I would follow him in his quest.

He did provide answers, revealing secrets, really— secrets of a world unknown to present mankind and answers that I had never considered. The answers only created more questions.

Walking this earth for so many years, I had become familiar with those not unlike myself.

Gelmir had called us the Immortals—men and women who never aged normally and were almost incapable of dying naturally. Not gods, but rather the eternal spirits of this earth, created by those who came in search of life and charged with the protection of the mortals residing here. Our mission was to protect them from the darkness that abounds in numerous forms, guarding our secrets carefully, so as not to be discovered. This necessitated moving from one place to the next, keeping our identities from those who could potentially harm the balance of this world.

In the past the darkness had deceived some into believing they were more than protectors of this earth and it inhabitants, but rather gods, given their gifts for the benefit of greed, power, and control.

They created an alliance with the darkness, and fell victim to its desires, which was nothing more than the beginning of the destruction of this world.

Those who did not follow the darkness perished at the hands of their brothers and sisters who had been deceived by it. The strongest was Karawan; he reined death and destruction on all who opposed him, not stopping until all who threatened his domination were eliminated.

Once there had been hundreds of us walking amongst the living mortals of this world, but we now dwindle in numbers. With the darkness taking over, many fled. A small group of warriors, the chosen twelve, remained with their families to fight to keep the human race alive.

The great wars had begun, and the fighting had become continuous. With their numbers few and their wills broken, nearly all hope had been lost, but for the strength of one. She had been willing to give all she had in order to see freedom for her family and peace amongst the races.

Her name was Alana. She was one of the twelve left behind to defend the human race. After a rather grueling battle, Karawan had captured her. Her life had been spared by the Dark Lord, but only because of her beauty and his desire to possess her completely.

As time passed, Alana, separated from her family but never forgetting her cause, convinced Karawan of her undying love and worship. Overcome by her unwavering devotion, Karawan faltered and fell under her mystical spell.

Given a rare opportunity, Alana placed the mighty Karawan in a sleep spell and imprisoned him in a chamber along with his followers. Her victory was not without losses and retribution, for the actions came swiftly.

Alana was struck down by the dark followers left behind who were not spelled by her, and she was lost to us. Unable to raise their leader from his slumber, and now so few in numbers, they ran, scattering to the winds, living for the day when they would be able to wake their leader and reap their revenge.

For decades now the Immortals have lived in peace, hiding amongst the human race in order to keep their identities a secret from the darkness that still lurks.

Of the twelve family leaders, only four original Immortals survived the great wars. The oldest of which was Gabriel. He, along with Isda, Ramiel, and Gelmir, now search for the descendents of our people, in the hopes that they may once again walk peacefully among the people of this world and stop the growing darkness that threatens to change our way of life.

Gelmir, one of the last surviving watchers of the original twelve, was entrusted with the task of finding the Chosen One. A descendent of the original twelve, the female child would be the savior of our kind and the inhabitants of this world. It was for that reason that he came to me.

I was born into a small gypsy family just south of New Orleans; our lives consisted of traveling from city to city, where we would set up camp, entertain the locals and sell our wares in the hopes of making enough money to survive another day.

This is how I learned to live off the land. My mother, Dina, was an Immortal; and she had been given the gift of sight. Her abilities had kept us safe and fed, for the most part. She could sense the wishes of those who entered the camp and knew what it was they wanted within moments of meeting them.

She was able to give them what they asked for and was paid for her services; but not all tolerated our kind, and it was not long before they came hunting for the witch who had tricked their family members.

Hidden in a hollowed tree by my mother and told to be silent, I watched as the angry mob entered our camp that fateful evening. I watched as my mother and family were taken from me; my future, as I knew it, was changed forever.

At seven years old I was alone. Any survivors left from the raid that evening had long since fled the territory, and with no family to speak of, I, a descendent of the Immortals, was lost.

With no knowledge of my true identity in this world, I moved through time and place thinking that I was nobody. I survived on pure instinct and the abilities that seemed to come to me so readily.

I was fast, faster than man and most animals. My eyesight was that of a hawk, and I had strength that outpowered the mightiest of beasts. I could hear for long distances, and if I concentrated, the faint sound of a rabbit scurrying miles away could be heard.

I knew that I was different. As I grew, the gifts became stronger. I turned to a life of crime, surviving on the skills that I had and living from day-to-day. I was alive, and finally, after a time, I found a home amongst the thieves with whom I worked.

Time would catch up with me eventually, as it does for any Immortal.

Not knowing I was Immortal, I was perplexed. I didn't age like my fellow mates, and when we got in a fight I usually healed faster than the others. My body's energy only got stronger when it should have been waning with age. I wouldn't be long before someone would see and know that I wasn't normal. I wasn't "human," and so the running began.

Every decade I created a new name, a new identity, a new life. I followed my own set of rules to never get caught. That was the mantra I lived by.

Knowing I was not like the average human, I began searching for clues in every new city I traveled. I carefully searched for something or someone who would know or understand where I had come from and who I was.

I spent years researching my kind, locating them one by one. Eventually, I found a total of five and we created a small Immortal family. It included Duncan, Mara, Shamus, James, and Tina.

We lived long lives, possessed special skills, and as a family we thrived. We were happy, all was good, and for a short period of time I was at peace. But like anything good in my life, it came to an end.

Adversity is an Immortal's life; not being able to live by the same standards or guidelines the mortal human has becomes a laborious duty. A duty not being able to fully understand, it can be rather baffling at times.

Some of us look at it as a challenge, one we were given to overcome. Others find the task of everyday living overwhelming and see the life of an Immortal as being forsaken, never being able to have the blessings of a normal life with families, children, and careers. They barely hold onto their fragile sanity and lose a little of themselves day-by-day.

The battle can be exhausting, and the aftermath is devastating. But the six of us, together, held tight and created something I had not had in some time—a family.

It wasn't until Seth came that I saw my beloved family change. We had stayed strong together; but slowly he insinuated himself into our lives, convincing those of us who were vulnerable with his ideas that we were different for a reason. Posing as a friend, he was accepted into our fold, unknowing of the treachery he would ultimately commit. The life I had worked so hard to create was fracturing in front of my eyes. One by one, they left; starting over, beginning anew, and searching for some form of normalcy in their lives. Some left in search of answers, hearing tales of the old ones who lived forever. They committed unimaginable deeds while hunting down answers, combing the continent for what Seth had called the Elders, in the hopes of finding them.

My small family was dispersed all over the world. Fractured and displaced, I tried to stay in touch, but

Seth's influences had turned the majority of my family away. All who were not with him were against him.

Seth had persuaded Mara easily; she had fancied herself in love with him and so had followed with her younger brother, Shamus, leaving only a small portion of my family somewhat intact.

Not sure of what to believe and ultimately being afraid, Duncan, James, and Tina left as well, searching for a promised life Seth had planted in their heads.

In the end, I was alone, and no better off than I had been before my little Immortal family began. Possibly it was worse, having lived for a brief time with the taste of what life could have been like, knowing the love of family.

Now I was broken, wandering, hurt, and bewildered as to the nature of who I was again and why I had been put on this earth.

What I was finding out, to my despair, was that I really didn't care. Eventually, I gave up. I settled for the routine of everyday life, praying I would not go insane and looking hopelessly for a day when my life would come to an end.

More decades went by with no sign of an end, a reprieve from the life I had found so difficult to live. I began conceiving of several ways to end my own life, only to be thwarted at every turn. I was stuck, with no release in sight.

At a crossroads, I had a choice to make. I couldn't kill myself and I couldn't continue living as I was. Convincing myself it was much safer being on my own and that I didn't need a family or even the answers I longed for about who I was, came to me easier than I had thought it would. It had been simple. I could go on living, just as I had been ... walking through life like a zombie and never caring about anything. Couldn't I?

Gelmir, coming into my life when he did, had salvaged any and all hope of understanding who and what I was. It had been Gelmir who had saved me from myself.

Over the last decade we have become great friends and comrades. Fighting together for what all Immortals left behind were created for, the protection of life on this planet and the return of order to our race. I have learned much under his guidance, and have become a strong warrior. Understanding the abilities that were gifted to me as a young Immortal was difficult, but with Gelmir's assistance, I learned how to use them properly and now know that they are invaluable.

Years of enhancing my gifts while we continued with the gathering only showed me the strength with which my ancestors had blessed me. Over time, I embraced the fact that I was Immortal, no longer wishing for a different life, one that had been my dream for so long. Protecting Gelmir in his quest for the Chosen One was my new life; I was a warrior, an Immortal with a cause, and I was happy for the most part.

My happiness was not without cost. Gelmir was one of the original Immortals of the twelve, and he has lived hundreds of years. Battle worn and exhausted over time in our search for the Chosen One has weakened him, the evidence of it shows in his strength of mind and body. I fear that if we don't find the Chosen One soon, the battle may be lost and the war will begin.

Eight

Alessar

Standing now in Gelmir's tiny house, I took a visual inventory of my surroundings. It was something I had learned to do over the years so as to protect myself against those who would see me dead.

It was an older house, built in the early eighteen hundreds, shortly after I was born. The front room was sparsely furnished; the only sign of recent life was the book that had been left open on a side table next to remnants of what looked to be Gelmir's lunch.

Glancing around the small home, I could see the entrance to the kitchen and a short hallway that led to the sleeping rooms in the back of the house. The front room was small and obviously served as a library.

The walls of the tiny room were covered in shelving from the ground up. They, in turn, held more books than I had ever seen in one small space. The weight of numerous books had bowed the shelving. They had overflowed some time ago and were now spilling onto the floor in stacks of hundreds or more.

The room's furnishing was sparse, to say the least. There was a leather armchair next to the side table where Gelmir had just eaten his lunch while reading. A few antiques occupied space in the room, looking as if they had been misplaced some time ago.

Mounted on the wall above the doorjamb was a Springfield musket; I knew it well. I had been issued one exactly like it during the War Between the States. Serving in the Arkansas Cavalry Third Regiment, I had killed many men with a gun identical to the one mounted there.

Sitting in the corner and piled with several more books was a dust-covered, worn settee and a glass cabinet. The cabinet held strange-looking tools or artifacts; they looked to be of Native origin, but I could not be sure. Turning from the glass cabinet, I paced to the kitchen. There was a back door that led directly into the forest behind the home. I stepped though the door and hollered again.

"Gelmir, are you out here?" Impatiently I waited for an answer, but nothing came. Scanning the small back-yard, nothing looked out of place. The edge of forest was only ten feet away, and it surrounded the house on all three sides.

It looked as if a notch had been cut from the forest floor and the tiny house was set inside, within its protective walls. The landscape was beautiful; the trees hugged the mountains that moved to the north and south of the house. Green plant life was everywhere; carpet moss covered the ground, rock, and trees. Lady ferns, with their light green foliage, dotted the landscape.

But it was the Guelder rose with its delicate blossom that gave the surroundings a feeling of home. The small clearing in front of the house was only visible when you broke through the tree line, protected by the forest walls and the deciduous plant life living within it.

The only sign there was life back here was the dirt trail leading to the entrance of the clearing. If you didn't know the tiny house was here, you would never be able to find it. Turning around, I decided to wait for Gelmir's return inside the house.

It began softly, a tinkle of chimes, a gentle whisper in the air. I closed my eyes and concentrated on the sound and the direction from which it was coming. It was miles away, to the north, calling me. I concentrated hard, listening for the sound again. Was it calling my name?

There it was again, "Alessar." Yes, it was calling my name; I began advancing toward the whisper.

It was louder, now that I had come closer. I could hear the sounds of song, words I didn't understand, yet there was something vaguely familiar. It was something or someone from my past.

It was my mother; her voice was in the air, singing a lullaby from my childhood. I ran faster, chasing the voice in the wind. I was almost there, bursting through the trees several at a time. I was racing blindly toward the edge of the forest floor where the trees ended and the sharp drop off of a cliff began. I stopped myself before plummeting to my ultimate death just at the edge of the cliff. I listened as her voice drew distant. She was leaving me. I could hardly hear her.

I reached deep within myself, concentrating, desperate to catch just one more note.

"Alessar." The whisper was there again, but this time it was not in the wind, but in my mind. "Can you hear me, Alessar? I have finally found you, my child. Come to me so that we may be together at last." I could feel the warmth of my mother's touch surrounding me; she was there, holding me in her arms and singing. It was beautiful, she was beautiful, and I was entranced, mesmerized by her song. Floating, as if dancing in the clouds, we moved together in sequence toward the heavens. Then it was dark.

Pain, excruciating pain, filled my head. I reached up and could feel the swelling of what would surely be an enormous bump, along with what felt like a crevasse in my scull. Still oozing blood in a sticky stream, I placed my hand on it to stifle the flow.

I was on the ground, the forest floor was under my cheek, and the smell of earth was strong. Opening my eyes, I blinked at the pain and knew my suspicions were correct. The moisture from the wet moss that lay beneath me was now leaching through my clothing. Blinking again, I could see the beginnings of what looked to be the forest wall. Blinking once more, I saw Gelmir; he was sitting on a large rock formation to the left of me. Fighting through the pain, I stumbled to a stand.

"What the hell happened?" I managed to get out.

"I believe that Golda was working her talents on you," Gelmir replied. He sat peacefully on his perch, as I tried to grasp what it was he was saying.

"What? Who the hell is Golda?" I asked.

"She is Abaddon's mistress, and I believe she was manipulating your thoughts and doing a very good job at it." He stood from his seated position and walked to place his hand upon my head. "Sorry about the knot on your head, but I had to knock you out in order to gain control."

"You did this to me?" I questioned, not quite sure as to the reason why.

"I had to; she was obviously convincing you of something and luring you to your death." I watched as he walked to the edge of the cliff and looked down. "If I had not come along when I did, you would be dead at the bottom of the cliff right now."

I followed his line of vision and knew he was right; the cliff was only a few feet from where I found myself lying on the ground when I awoke. I stood, staring at what could have been my final resting place, and was now thankful for the throbbing bump the size of a golf ball on my head.

"Golda is very good with her talents; she can make anyone believe they are hearing or seeing their heart's desire or their worst fears."

Still standing and looking over the edge, Gelmir placed a hand on my shoulder and asked, "So, Alessar, what is your heart's desire?"

I turned to him and questioned, "What makes you think she had my desire and not my fears?"

"I have lived a long time, Alessar. I know what happiness looks like on a man's face, and you were happy just now as you danced around, looking for whatever it was she had you convinced of. So tell me, what was it?"

Shaking my head, I smiled. I knew I looked the fool, "My mother's voice, singing," I replied.

"Well, you have a better understanding of what it is we are dealing with. Abaddon has several Immortals with special powers and talents available to him. He will continue with his destruction of this world as long as no one stands in his way." He turned from the cliff edge and walked toward the forest wall. "You need to be aware of what you are up against and be prepared for the worst."

He turned back to look at me as I followed. "We are the last of our kind. Without us, all hope will be lost, and this world will perish as we know it."

I watched as he turned and disappeared into the forest. Shaking my now tender head, I followed.

"Hey, Gelmir, you're a little heavy on the drama, don't you think?"

"Really? I don't think so. After all, you were the one that almost took a fatal step listening to your dead mother's voice."

"Okay, point taken," I conceded.

"Abaddon only has enough strength, at this point, to influence the people of power running this world. The ultimate power would come if he were to control all the Immortals and the Chosen One, the true child.

This is why we search for her ourselves, opposing him at every turn, hoping we can one day return peace to the Immortals and continue with our work of watching over this world and its inhabitants."

I continued to follow Gelmir in silence, absorbing everything that he had said. Finally seeing a break in the forest wall, I knew we were close to being back at the tiny house he called home.

Arriving at the back door of the dwelling, Gelmir turned and said, "Alessar, our journey is changing. It is becoming much more dangerous. You need to understand that the risks are great and there is a good possibility that one or both of us may not survive."

"Again, with the drama." Smiling and placing my hand on his shoulder, I looked into his eyes and assured him I understood.

"I understand, Gelmir. Life is nothing more than a merry-go-round if you are not living it to the fullest. So, my good friend and teacher let us live life now and find ourselves the Chosen One."

"Well then, my good and brave friend let us begin today's quest."

Nine

Dylan

The sounds of voices speaking were rapping at my numb senses. Vaguely I could hear Mrs. T speaking. She was talking to someone, but I didn't know who. I willed my fuzzy mind to hear and understand what was happening, and her voice became clearer.

"Damn it, Gelmir! I knew this would happen. She is not ready; she is just beginning to see her gifts. If we pressure her, we run the risk of losing the only Collective Immortal that we know of."

"We have no other choice, Emily. It is time. The Chosen child is now among us, and we need to find her, before Abaddon does."

I could feel my senses returning slowly. The feeling of cold tile beneath my weary body, the smell of food cooking on the stove: slowly reality was coming back. I listened to the voices speaking again. First Mrs. T or "Emily" as the man called her. She was upset and speaking of losing something. Then I heard my name, and the mystery man was speaking. Then another name, one I didn't know, "Abaddon." The name made my skin crawl, as if I almost knew who it was they were referring too, but not quite.

Who was this man she was speaking with? Why was I on the floor? What was happening? My head was fuzzy. I searched the corners of my mind, and there it was—the orb, the strange man sitting across from Mrs. T, the pictures of my childhood and then the pictures of my death. I squeezed my eyes shut, locking out the visions that were flashing in my mind, hurling more information at me than I wanted.

Struggling to gain control, I concentrated on something else. I began to sense the warmth of another. Arms, strong and muscular, were wrapped around me, holding me in place. My other senses began to take over, and the smell of soap and leather mixed with a little sandalwood became obvious, and then another vision. Racing across my mind were the feelings of warmth, caring, protection; I was safe in these arms.

With my eyes closed, I wrapped my arms around my chest and shifted into the warmth, snuggling into the arms that held me.

Then more visions invaded my head; this time it was fascination, attraction, and finally lust, pure sexual wantonness.

My eyes slammed open, only to see a beautiful set of chocolate brown eyes staring back at me, with what could only be considered concern residing in their depths.

It was him, the man from the street, the one I had almost run into with my bike. He was looking at me, and I was staring at him, up close and very personal.

I could see more of him now than I had before on the street. The man I had found attractive at a distance was now holding me in his arms.

My body shifted deeper into his warmth. Classically handsome was the only way to describe him—chiseled features, straight nose, and jet-black hair to his shoulders. He was what some women would call "eye candy," and I was devouring every inch of him.

Moving over his face, across the wide breadth of his shoulders, down his chest, my eyes slowly caressed ever inch. Then his voice came to me, and I began to melt at its soft timber.

"Keep looking at me like that, sweet thing, and I may have to ask the Elders to leave."

The reality of what he was saying was delayed due to my overly clouded mind. I searched for understanding, and when it came, it was too late. I had already involuntarily smoothed my hands over his chest and purred in my throat like a wanton she-cat. I watched as my hand moved ever so slowly across his chest and then a vision of him, naked in all his glory, flashed though my mind and was gone in an instant.

Reality snapped me out of my stupor. Looking back into his eyes, I saw desire and lust had replaced the concern that had been there only moments before.

Mortified, I scrambled to get to my feet. Now standing, I tried to grasp what had just happened and found myself falling short of any answers.

Taking in my surroundings and absorbing any and all information I could see, only bewilderment set in and I fell back on the old reliable that I had used for years when something strange would happen and I didn't understand what it was.

Clutching my head in my hands, I closed my eyes and reached out into my consciousness; grasping the far corners of my mind, I probed, looking for answers from the occupants now crowding the tiny country kitchen.

Instantly I froze, no longer probing for answers, but feeling a sense of something else. It was him, the older man seated at the table. He wasn't looking at me, but staring directly out the window into the backyard of Mrs. T's home. Somehow he was there, in my mind, reading my thought, or was I reading his? Without verbalizing a single word, I probed again.

"Can you hear me?" I posed the question, not sure if I was going mad. But I needed to know if what I was hearing or feeling was real. Normally when I went looking for answers, they were right there on the edge of my mind. People were easy to read, some more than others, as if they wanted to speak, but held back out of fear.

For years I hid my ability to see the pictures and thoughts residing in people's minds. This was mostly for my own protection, for I had been too young when I discovered the gift and didn't know how to use it. The thoughts people have can sometimes be very confusing and, for a young child, even disturbing.

So I had pushed it away, locked it down in the corners of my mind. I can remember distinctly the day I brought it back into my life. I was in high school. Not being one of the most popular girls, I had few friends; but I was happy. I had my family and my job at the shop with Mack. Life, in general, was good.

The day my gift came back was the day I saw her. Charlotte was a new girl to my school; she had just transferred and had only been there for about a month. She was walking across campus, and the feelings of despair, pain, and loneliness hit me so hard that my stomach clenched and I was sure I would throw up.

Not exactly sure what was happening, I decided to follow her and introduce myself. I knew something was wrong and I had to stop the feeling I was getting from her. So I insinuated myself into her life, and it wasn't long before Charlotte and I became good friends.

I came to understand a little more about that first day, the day I had felt so many horrible feelings coming from her, for she had been contemplating suicide.

Her family had been shattered by the loss of her mother, and any stability she'd had before her mother's death was now gone. Living in an abusive household with a father who drank the majority of the time he was awake, she had been lost. After a rather horrific night hiding in a closet to get away from her father, she had decided she couldn't go on any longer. She would finally be with her mother.

We only spoke of it the one time. I didn't need her to elaborate; I already knew why she had changed her mind. And for some reason, she understood I knew more than she could ever tell me.

Since that fateful day, I no longer blocked the feelings or pictures I received from people willingly. I did have rules. I wouldn't poke around in people's heads unless I had to. I didn't need to know more than I already did, but in most situations the information is just sitting there ready to be given up and consumed. But this was different. He was like no other I had ever felt. He was strong, pulling at me and then he was there in my mind, seeing everything I could see.

The jolt of energy hit me hard, like a sharp jab to the gut. My stomach clenched, and the answer I had been waiting for came with the turning of his head. The mystery man was looking directly at me and using the same nonverbal actions I was. He responded to my question.

"Yes!" Crystal blue eyes pierced my thoughts in answer. "Just as you can hear me, Dylan."

Everything went white and then dark; I was falling and then I was soaring. *What's happening to me?* I was still awake, but everything I looked at was blurred, cloudy, or fuzzy; strange.

I could hear Mrs. T. She was speaking to the man sitting at the table, but she was leaning over someone. Someone was lying on the floor. I looked closer and shuttered at what I was seeing.

It was me. I was lying on the floor again, but yet I wasn't.

I could see their concern at my passed-out body, Mrs. T and the man who had held me earlier. They were speaking to me and I could hear them, but it was as if they were not in the same room. Rather that they were a long distance away or possibly in a different room, and their voices were having a difficulty carrying though the plaster of the walls. Muffled, yes, that was it; the sound of their voices was muffled. Why?

All but him, he was there again, speaking to me, clear as a bell. I could see he was still seated at the table, and yet his voice seemed to be coming from right beside me, it was so clear. Turning toward the sound of his voice, he was there floating, in front of me like a ghostly vision.

"Dylan, don't you think it would be wise to join the rest of the party back in the real world?" His voice was strong, but his body had become some kind of corporal being.

"Who are you? Am I dead?" I whispered softly, or so I thought. But rather than coming from my lips in the form of words, it came out of my mind once again, but this time it was less foggy. Pieces were starting to fit together. I could see that I was lying on the floor of Mrs. T's kitchen.

The handsome man who had held me earlier had once again taken up the vigil of holding my prone body off the cold tile floor. Mrs. T was sitting on the floor across from him, speaking to me, assuring that all would be well. The mystery man was still sitting at the table, and yet somehow, he was also floating with me. Both of us were hovering over the scene that was slowly unfolding beneath us. Gently he shook his head in answer to my question.

"Who are you? What's happening to me? Why am I here?" Searching for the answers, I looked to the mystery man's corporal being, and questioned him again.

"All will be understood in time, Dylan." He was being vague, and for some reason I knew that it was on purpose. As if he wanted me to figure it out on my own.

"As for now, I really think it would be in your best interest if you went back to your body and rested. It is not good for one as young as you to be out of the body without understanding the limits it has on the physical being."

Observing from my spectral view, directly over the room in which my prone body lay in the arms of a stranger, I gathered enough strength to move. Once a hovering form, I had now closed the gap and stood on the ground next to Mrs. T.

Curiosity had gotten the better of me, and I needed to see more, feel more, experience more. The closer I got to my own body, the weaker I felt.

Moving away from my body and toward the man seated at the table, I felt different. A strange new source of strength became known to me. It was drawing my aura, pulling at me, wanting me to absorb it.

I needed more, it was drawing me in, directing me to discard my well-known protective barriers and grasp at the newly found information that was becoming easier to access in the form I was now in. I could block the unwanted information with little or no pain at all.

Before, enduring the pain of unwanted information from another's mind could be excruciating and settle me with days of migraines. So rarely did I ever dig deep into the minds of strangers or absorb anything that was not already out there for the taking.

This was different, though. I could feel everything, see everything, and there was no pain, just light—ribbons and ribbons of light, like the ones that I observed coming from the orb. Turning, I looked to Mrs. T.

I saw ribbons of light all around her. They were long beautiful strips of light of her thoughts, memories, and her whole life being. It was beautiful.

The man on the floor holding my body had them too. I probed to see his more clearly, and new degrees of energy and power began to wash over and into me. It was as if a new, delicious food had just been introduced into my diet in the form of light; I savored each tasty bite.

It was not that dissimilar to what the orb had demonstrated and displayed earlier, but this new source of light was one of direct power. I began to inhale its essence, feeling the strength of the ribbon wrap around my body, filling me; slowly the feeling of power engulfed me. I was strong, stronger than I had ever felt.

New degrees of understanding were being displayed in front of my very eyes. Knowledge and history that had once been hidden away, I now understood. It was intoxicating, and I was drowning in the swell of information he had offered up so willingly.

"Stop it, Dylan. You're not strong enough yet, and it is against the rules of our kind. You may not continue with your course of action without permission." He was there again, standing beside me, but this time he was not cloudy or fuzzy looking. He was no longer a spectral being, but was back to his whole form, and this time he was talking to me directly for all to hear. I watched as Mrs. T became confused and questioned him.

"Gelmir, what are you doing? The girl is passed out from the shock of what she saw." She was staring at him as if he had lost his mind; he had, after all, been looking up into thin air when he had spoken to me.

Gelmir reached out and touched her shoulder; as if awakened from a slumber, she shook the confusion from her eyes and was looking at me too. Again he spoke.

"Dylan, stop what you are doing and return to your body. I know you are confused and don't understand what's happening, but if you don't stop soon, you will end up hurting Alessar." His gaze shifted from me and went to the man who was still holding my lifeless body. The man who had been so handsome and sexy before was now contorted with pain, straining every muscle, and I was causing it.

It was the ribbons; I was draining him. I had to let go. I pushed away and they snapped. His body, once tense with stress and pain, was now relaxed and slumped in relief.

I was floating again, going farther and farther away from my body. I wanted to go back, but it was so nice, not having to be bound down. I tried again, but to no avail.

I was losing ground, moving away from my body rather than getting closer. His name was Gelmir; that is what Mrs. T had called him. Who was he?

The air shifted and he was back with me. This time he was speaking so that only I could hear him. It was more of a bellow. He screamed at my inner being, grabbing my attention.

"Dylan Merrin Ella, daughter of Isda Ella the Collective, I command you to stop this moment."

The air shifted again, and I became a semi-solid form, somewhere between what I had once been as a ghostly substance, to a stronger, more stable form. Held together by what, I was not sure, but I was no longer cloudy and fuzzy, yet not completely whole either.

I had split in two, with one half of my body lying on the ground totally unaware, and the other half floating around the room, wanting nothing more than to find an outlet of energy I could absorb.

Suspended in air, I fought to gain control, struggling against an unseen force. Then he was there again, as a ghostly spirit, his real form sitting back in the kitchen chair.

I posed the questions to myself mentally: what was happening and who the hell was this man? It was the man in question who answered.

"Gelmir. That is my name, and the other man who sits and holds your body is Alessar. We are your family; you can trust us, Dylan. Now let go."

The air around me shifted again. This time the feeling of a gentle pressure began prodding me in the direction of my prone body, lying in the arms of the man he called Alessar, not three feet away from my goal. A strong, inner battle was being waged; I wanted to return to my body, but it was difficult.

I was being pulled in a different direction. It wasn't until the sharp pain stabbed through my entire being that I began to panic. I was dying, and I would never be able to see my family again.

"Take a deep breath; move over your body and concentrate, concentrate on the whole of your body." I followed his instructions and began to concentrate as he had asked; step-by-step he guided me toward the ultimate goal.

"Now, slowly lay down and consume the emptiness that lies just there, deep inside your body beneath all the flesh and bone where the soul lies."

Slowly, I lie down and felt the warmth envelope my entire being; I was back, whole once again. Completely drained, I tried to open my eyes but knew that it would be no use. Reaching out one more time with my mind, I felt him again.

"What is happening to me?" I begged.

"Rest, Dylan; I will explain everything when you wake up."

I followed my surroundings with my mind and felt the man who had been holding me, gently pick me up and carry me out to the living room. At Mrs. T's request, he placed me on the sofa. She proceeded to gather a blanket and cover me, tucking the blanket in around my entire body. I felt it as she lovingly pushed the unruly hair back from my forehead and brushed a light kiss across my brow.

"Sleep well, little one. You are going to be just fine."

Not sure what exactly had taken place in the last ten minutes, but feeling completely drained, I trusted the fact that I felt safe and secure lying on Mrs. T's sofa, so I slept. I was completely unaware of the turmoil I had just created with my short little jaunt into the other world.

Ten

Alessar

"What the hell was that, Gelmir?" Trying to scream with what little strength was left in my body, my aggravation came out as only a low grumble. Which was okay, considering she, the beauty we had come for, was now fast asleep on the couch in the other room.

"So, when were you going to stop her from sucking the life right out of me? Before or after I had little or no strength left to survive?" Walking directly up to Gelmir, I could see the strain in his eyes and understood that he was worried about the obvious problems ahead of us. She was stronger than he had anticipated.

He was seated in the kitchen chair that he had occupied earlier, but this time his body was slumped and he was looking very old. Concern quickly replaced the anger that had been filling my body only moments ago, and an overwhelming feeling of protection came over me.

"Gelmir, are you all right?" Laying my hand on his shoulder, I felt him recoil into his body, as if he were in pain; quickly I removed the pressure of my hand and sat beside him.

Gelmir had been with me for almost more than a decade now. That may not seem long for many, but in our new line of work, it could be considered a lifetime. If Immortals could have what is called a lifetime.

It had taken months for me to open up and trust him. Over the years, with several journeys and battles behind us, I had learned to trust Gelmir with my life. He was my only family, and for this Immortal, to even consider having a family was a leap of faith.

I had learned a great deal about trust and respect under Gelmir's tutelage, and seeing him strained like this was difficult.

In the beginning when Gelmir and I had first met, he had been strong and healthy. Over time, I have watched as that strength has slowly been stripped from him.

Most believe that an Immortal cannot die, hence the word Immortal, meaning everlasting and eternal. However, that is not exactly true.

Immortal beings such as Gelmir, myself, and others, whom we have been searching for, are capable of death. We are subjected to the same basic principles of life and death as that of a mortal being.

If we are struck by sword or knife, we bleed; if a bullet penetrates our body, we can be mortally wounded. Only we have the strength and gift of powers that sustain our lives longer and stronger than that of a mortal man.

Unnatural death can take us at any time if we are not prepared and, of course, if we choose to go; then we forfeit any life left with a healthy spirit.

When the life force is driven from the body of an Immortal, the spirit dies, leaving behind only a shell of a being, one who can be manipulated by a stronger being.

Gelmir and I have seen many Immortals in battle who have been taken this way. Struck down, no longer living and not really dead, they are a slave to the dark side. We seek them out and end what life they have left. In doing so, a small part of Gelmir is lost with them, aging him with each release he grants.

Looking at him now, you would have thought that he had released the souls of an army in battle, not guiding a wisp of a girl no more than twenty-three years of age.

She had done this to me. She had pierced my mind and soaked up my inner thoughts and energy easily; she was stronger than I had thought possible. Gelmir had blocked most of the attack, but a good portion of it had reached though and ripped away at my mind. If Gelmir hadn't been there, I shuddered to think what would have happened.

Understanding dawned, and I reached for Gelmir once again; this time, gently applying the healing palm of my hand to his shoulder.

"Emily, I believe that Gelmir requires rest." I looked to her, and understanding dawned for her as well.

"Follow me, Alessar. We will lie him down in the guest room. I believe he will be comfortable there." She moved down the small hallway leading to the bedrooms and bath, and entered the first door on the right. Concern had shown heavily on her face when she turned to watch Gelmir and I follow.

Tenderly, I guided Gelmir to stand. Once standing, together we navigated the small dwelling and entered behind Emily into the spare bedroom. Gelmir lie down and briefly spoke before falling into a deep sleep.

"Alessar, watch over her and don't let her go far. We opened a window tonight, and she will have questions." He held my hand while Emily covered him with a blanket. He looked so fragile; I had never seen him this weak. Smiling, he closed his eyes and spoke once again.

"She is strong, Alessar. She will be a great asset for the battle that comes. Watch over her and make sure she is safe." His eyes fluttered open, and he looked deeply, before closing them again and falling into a deep, resounding sleep.

Walking from the room and entering the hallway, Emily stated that she would go over and visit Dylan's family to quell any worries they might have due to her absence at home.

Following her into the small living room, I watched as she checked on Dylan and then proceeded to exit the front door, bound for the Black residence. I heard the concern in her voice as she spoke though the screen door she had gently closed behind her.

"I'll be back shortly. Make yourself at home. I believe you will be here for at least the evening." Her footfalls sounded against the wood decking as she stepped down and headed away from the house.

Alone, I gathered what little strength I had and walked to the overstuffed chair sitting in the corner of the small living room opposite of the sofa. I had a clear view of the girl and the hallway leading to Gelmir.

Who was this girl? How was she stronger than an experienced and ancient Immortal such as Gelmir? Over time, I had come to understand through Gelmir's teachings that Immortals came in several shapes, sizes, and strengths.

Some were healers, not unlike Gelmir. But he was much more; his talents ranged farther than the average Immortal. Then again, Gelmir had lived longer than most other Immortals and had educated himself in the mystical arts.

Where there had once been hundreds of thousands of us, we now dwindle in numbers. Our talents ranged from Elementors to Collectors. Elementors are those capable of manipulating the elements around us, such as wind, water, fire, and earth. They also have the ability to speak with the animals in nature, creating an understanding between species when necessary. Emily was blessed with this gift.

Then there were Watchers, immortals who could see the future and predict with precision what was to come. Several had multiple talents in order to survive, but never more than that of a Collector.

Sitting in the small living room of Emily's house, a trusted ally to the cause, and with a slumbering Gelmir only a room away, I had to wonder. Was the young girl who silently slept on the sofa across the room exactly that?

A Collector was an immortal with the ability to seize gifts from other immortals, and then use those gifts for their own benefit. If so, she would be a valuable asset after she was trained how to use her gift, or a horrible mistake, should the darkness ever reach her.

Collectors were one of the strongest immortals I knew of. Their abilities outweighed any other immortal due to the fact that they could shift their bodies and minds to absorb any and all abilities that were gifted to them.

If an Immortal gifted a Collector with their abilities, then a token would be given, and with that token came all the knowledge of how to use the abilities of that gift. So not only could she hold the talents of a Healer, she could also have the talents of a Traveler or any ability that she was gifted with, even that of a Guardian.

However, if the Dark Lords were ever to get hold of her, she would be trained to strip every gift and ability from her victims without even a single worry as to the damage she was doing to the Immortal. When ability is given, it is given freely by the Immortal; but when it is stripped away, damage is done. A Collector can take too much and eventually leave the Immortal they are touching completely destroyed.

Not many Collectors were left. In fact, the last Gelmir and I had known, there had been only three in existence. If she were one that would mean that there were now four; and her potential could level the playing fields, if she were to be united with our cause. Only time would tell if she would follow in her ancestors' footsteps and join us in our quest against the darkness.

I studied the sleeping form of the young lady and cringed at the thought that she may go the other direction.

"What the hell have we gotten ourselves into this time, Gelmir?" Running a hand through my hair, I leaned back and waited for Emily's return.

Eleven

Alessar

The small house was quiet and calm, with a few natural creaking noises coming from here and there. That was to be expected in a house so old. For the most part, it was peaceful. Always being alert had become a necessity in this new world of danger and never-ending turmoil. This made it difficult to relax, let alone feel comfortable enough to completely rest. Taking the opportunity to close my eyes was something I hadn't been able to do in quite some time and feel completely safe.

Since the first day Gelmir walked into my life, I was prepared for the worst. I was already at odds with the world I lived in, but nothing compared to what I lived in now. The difference now was that I had a reason, a cause for the turmoil. Not that I didn't have enough problems already, I was an Immortal with no known history of family or heritage and wanted nothing more than a piece of just that to call my own.

Gelmir had eased some of the memories of who I was with information on my family, giving me a sense of worth I had been searching for, for some time. However, no amount of answers could still the troubled memories of a small boy who had spent the majority of his life searching for the tattooed man who killed his mother.

She had been the only person I could remember who had ever cared for me unconditionally, showing me the love I still longed for today. I had been so young when the tattooed man had come into the encampment and massacred the only family life I knew.

After the massacre, I had searched for help, but it would be days before it arrived. Another traveling family showed me little kindness, but rather used me as a slave, after they took me in. But I endured and vowed that I would find the man who had brought this pain into my young life, and I would kill him, avenging my mother's death.

Years passed, and it would be nothing to say that times had been rough as a young boy; but with great perseverance, I carried myself through and into manhood.

When I finally gained the strength to strike out on my own, I began my search. Over time I prospered in both strength and knowledge, making myself a formidable man; yet I failed regularly in finding the one thing I desired the most: my past, my history, my ancestors, my family, or anything having to do with who I was. My entire life, I had searched for family.

Finding a makeshift family of Immortals over time had satisfied me for a while, but even that family had been taken from me. I had finally come to terms with never knowing who I really was and if there was anyone out there whom I could call family, when Gelmir entered my life.

Now I had the information I needed, in some ways much more than I had ever wanted.

Gelmir had shown me my family history from the book of linage that I carried with me at all times.

It had spoken of my mother, Dina, and my father, Terrell, and the birth of their one and only child, Alessar Keane Belmonte of the family Guardian. I thought back to that first month and everything I learned about the immortals.

"Gelmir, what does this mean? 'The family Guardian?'" I asked, looking to him, seated in his old leather wing-back chair.

"Hmm. What did you say, son?" Gelmir replied, pushing the fallen hair from his eyes.

"In the book of lineage, it says that I was born into the family Guardian; what does that mean?" I asked, looking to him for answers.

"Oh, you mean your clan or tribe name." Slowly Gelmir closed the book he was reading and went into a description or story of sorts, of what the family Guardian meant.

As a Guardian, or as some called themselves Warriors or even Knights, it was our job to protect the source.

The source was the bible of the Prime. It contains any and all research, data, experiments, and information that our creators and ancestors had gathered and kept of our creation, along with the creation of powers unknown to most Prime and man.

No one but the original twelve knew of the source's exact location after the exodus. Not even they had the power to gain the source without all twelve present.

It was for the protection of the Prime and the human race to keep such raw power hidden, locked away until the day it would be necessary to use it, and then only when it was safe for the Prime creators to return to Earth and live their lives in peace.

One key was given to each of the Prime who were honored to defend this world. Only when all twelve keys were brought together did the master key form and show the location of the source. This would bring back the creator of the Prime and allowing peace to reign amongst all, for the next millennium to come.

However, many of the original twelve were gone now, fallen in battle or turned by the Darkness. Along with the loss of eight of the original twelve, came the loss of their keys. Over time, battles had been waged for the ownership of the keys. Their rightful owners gone and the keys stolen, darkness had consumed much, and many keys had fallen into the Dark Lords' hands.

With possession of six keys, the battle of domination was half won. Should the darkness prevail in finding the other two keys that had been lost over time during the many battles fought, the swing of power would shift, and the ravaging would begin again.

In order to retrieve the wealth of power from the source, Karawan had waged wars against his own kind for decades. Gaining control of six keys and searching for the other two that were lost had been his immediate goal.

His undoing had come when he had tried to gain control of Alana's key. She had thwarted him, and after he had fallen under her spell, she had used the last of her strength to hide her key, before succumbing to death.

The final four, the last of the original twelve still in possession of their keys, had gone into hiding for fear of losing them. Should all twelve ever be captured by the darkness, no hope would be left for peace amongst the Prime or the human race.

Alana had trapped Karawan with his own greed; the possession of her spirit had been his downfall. He and the majority of his following had been captured, suspended in life, unaware of their surroundings, and in a continuous deep sleep.

However, not all were captured; some had escaped. They had gone into hiding, waiting for the day they could rise up again and release their leader, Karawan, and defeat the creators and the human race.

"This is not the end of the story, young Alessar." I smiled at the memory of Gelmir's enthusiasm when he told the story of the lost keys; he had looked so young then. "The four remain Prime had been given a reprieve by Karawan's slumber, this is true." He sighed at the memories of the distant past, "No longer battling daily, the searching for the lost keys has only intensified."

"The six keys that Karawan had sequestered with one of his minions before his capture still elude us. However, we have successfully retrieved one of the two still at large." Glancing at the back of his hand, he stared at the light scar gracing its surface.

"Alana's is yet to be found." Glancing my way, then slightly nodding at his now opened book, he indicated with a finger a single passage within. Continuing on, Gelmir said, "It is written that in the last days, before the exodus began, and before the twelve were chosen, a gathering of the elder creators was made." Looking up from the writings, he continued on.

"There is nothing here in these writings of its purpose; however, some say that the elder creators came together and with their joint power, established the prophecy. The same prophecy that you and I have worked so hard to see fulfilled." Sighing, he closed the book and handed it to me.

"I have more to do. Educate yourself, Alessar; these books hold your history."

Clutching the book in my hand, I watched as he moved across the room. He paused only long enough to give me a final strange look before exiting the house out the back door.

After Gelmir had handed me the book, I wondered about that look he had given me, along with the change in his demeanor right before he had left. At the time, I had shrugged it off as him being preoccupied with thoughts of the past. I wished now that I had taken the time to ask what was bothering him. Maybe it would have helped in understanding what was happening in that vast mind of his. Instead, I had reconciled my slight worry and devoured every book I could get a hold of.

It was important for me to understand who the Prime were, what they meant to me, and how I fit into the entire picture. I started where Gelmir had left off.

During the gathering, they had not only chosen the final twelve who would stay behind and fight for the freedom of their race and mankind, but it was also rumored that the creators had established a failsafe, just as Gelmir had eluded to.

Gelmir was at the gathering, and he had been chosen as one of the twelve. One of the younger immortals at the time, he was chosen for his many talents and gifts. He was strong and trustworthy, but not privy to the knowledge held by the elder of the twelve, Alana. It would be years before he would learn of the prophecy. Only then would he dedicate himself to the knowledge and fulfillment of it.

Gelmir had scoured the earth looking for remnants of the Prime's past. Books and records from the Prime historians had been lost centuries earlier due to the great wars. Battle had seen most of what was left behind during the exodus of the Creators destroyed and the few remaining records that were left had been hidden for safety in the capable hands of faithful human keepers.

The Prime's knowledge was handed down from generation to generation. Each new keeper was given instructions for the care of such important history. Bound in books and protected with their lives, the information was passed for centuries. Over time, the dedication by humans faltered, and the knowledge entrusted to them was forgotten.

Although it was almost impossible to find after centuries being lost, Gelmir searched for any information that would lead him to more history of the Prime and ultimately that of the prophecy. He had found a strong lead of such records in the journal of a human.

The woman's name was Teresa. She had served as a governess in one of the keeper's ancestral homes. Going though some old books, she discovered a large tome and found it very interesting. Within her journal she wrote of how the great book looked. Bound in leather and enclosed with straps, it was very old and worn. At first glance she had thought it to be a bible or possibly the history of the ancestral family she worked for. After closer inspection, she discovered that she couldn't be farther from the truth.

She described in her journal the writings that were strange and indiscernible within the sheaves of paper. She could not read the foreign words within the tome. It did, however, hold drawings of things, creatures, and places not of this world. That had been all that was needed to grab her attention. She had studied the book very carefully, turning over pages with gentle hands and making sure not to damage the already fragile documents.

She had just began going through the second portion that she had sectioned out earlier, when her employer came in and took the book away. He had been very upset with her and requested that she never touch it again. She had promised to do exactly that in order to keep her job. She didn't need to look at that book when there were several others she could read from. A few notes in her own personal journal about the book would never have been discovered, but Teresa had drawn some of the creatures she had seen within the pages of the leather bound book. That is what had gotten Gelmir's attention and given him the first taste of the hunt.

It would be years before Gelmir would find the book Teresa described within her journal. He made very little progress toward finding the tome until one day a Prime Seer by the name of Canton requested to see him. Standing in the inner most sanctum of Canton's stronghold, he told Gelmir of a vision that he had seen. He described a place in the old world where a vast amount of knowledge was buried deep underground, hidden by the watchful eye of darkness. He spoke of how he saw Gelmir there in the midst of this knowledge, holding the key to the future of the Prime. Describing his vision as carefully as he could, he was able to lead Gelmir to a chamber filled with information and documents describing the past and possible future.

The information would not come to Gelmir easily. Attempting to gain access to the chamber would be dangerous. The chamber itself was inside the home of a known Favored Prime, one who had been practicing with the dark arts for sometime. In his early years, his evil knew no bounds. He had taken lives at will and spared no one his wrath. Over the last few decades, it seemed he had lost interest in the human race and was sequestering himself within his home. Gelmir had no idea why he had become so uninterested. He only knew that he needed the information the Dark Favored possessed and would do anything to get it.

They entered the Dark Favored home during the high noon hour when his powers would be at their weakest. They fought the unbound evil that greeted them. The chamber hadn't been difficult to enter once the house was breached and the darkness of the Favored Prime dispatched. It had been a long and difficult battle, and a few good immortals were lost that day to the darkness watching over the chamber. Yet the much-needed history and documents recovered were worth the battle that was waged against the darkness. The Prime had won, but at a very heavy price.

With the document and papers now in Gelmir's possession, they were free to search and collect as much information on the prophecy as possible. It was a painstakingly long process that took several months. Eventually it led to more clues and more information about the prophecy. Over time the Seer Canton would have other visions, and then with as much detail as possible, he would guide Gelmir as close as he could to the knowledge he sought. Sometimes the visions that Canton would have led to a windfall of information, but more often than not, it was just a small treasure from the past.

Painstakingly, Gelmir would put together the pieces of the past, searching for the answers. Knowing that the Creators had left behind clues, he worked diligently to put them together. It was difficult work. Between the battles of good versus evil, he would struggle to gain what little knowledge he could of the prophecy so that one day it may be fulfilled.

Years would pass before I would help in the quest Gelmir had begun. It was during a rather bad uprising of the darkness that Gelmir and I had stumbled upon another book holding the stories of the Prime and their ultimate creation and destruction.

We had just finished battling a rather nasty Shape Shifter named Edmund. According to the testimony of the clergyman whom he had tortured for information, he had been terrorizing the locals of Ashbourne, looking for one of the lost keys. Other witness spoke of a book he held which described the lost key he searched for.

After the battle with Edmund had been won, Gelmir searched his belongings. Within them were several books. Included in one were the description of the keys in detail and the words of the prophecy stated in full. Several other rare and priceless Prime artifacts, capable of great power when used properly, were also included in his belongings. It was strange to see an underling with such a large wealth of knowledge and power at his fingertips.

This led Gelmir and I both to believe that the Shape Shifter Edmund had double crossed his Dark Master and stolen the newly found possessions. Edmund was known to work for a rather vicious Favored Prime. Thankfully it had been Gelmir and I who had found him, before his master did. Mercy would not be given to a thief inside the realm of darkness. He was uneducated in the dark arts like that of his master. Gelmir and I had inadvertently saved him from unimaginable pain and gained the much-needed secrets of the past.

The treasures Edmund had held were a great discovery. They gave us insight to the secrets of the past and what the future held. According to the writings, if the twelve left behind did not fulfill the task of overthrowing the darkness, a prophet would be born. A great Watcher had seen and spoken the prophecy after centuries of failed attempts by the original twelve to gain control.

According to the Watcher, a young female Prime, born to the world and orphaned at birth by her Immortal father, would be gifted with the power of Ultimate Creation. She would be marked behind the ear with a sign of the Creators.

Lost to her Immortal family, her human mother would raise her in hiding, concealing her true identity from all who would harm her. She would be the Chosen One, created by the Elders to lead our people to peace.

Some of the writings say that the creators, in the last days, had seen the falling of this world and that is why they ran. Others believe they knew that only with their absence would good defeat evil and peace prevail. With centuries passed, and finally foreseen by another Watcher, the Chosen One walks amongst us.

And so, we seek to find her and bring an end to the constant battling that has become a part of this world. The darkness seeks her too, in order to convert her and gain the ultimate power.

Yet, even with all that we now know, I wonder at the wisdom and power of sight. A Watcher can predict the future, but the future can be changed. Where was the insight into the future before? Couldn't the Creators have predicted the betrayal that was made by the Favored Prime and stopped it from happening?

What had they done? They had given birth to the Prime and from that, the evil that now resides all over the planet. Not completely sure of what we were doing here, I turned to Gelmir for consideration.

I had been striving to understand for some time who and what I was. Gelmir had given me what I needed, and I had grown under his careful tutelage. He had educated and trained me. Gracing me with an understanding of what the Prime were and why the Creators had made us, but was it enough to continue on, trying to understand why they didn't just stop it? If they had, would my mother still be alive?

She had been killed by an Immortal, the tattooed man named Jericho; he had been one of the original twelve. Only he had been weak and the darkness that Karawan wielded turned him against his kind.

The same original twelve who were to have saved our species had failed me. It was for that reason that I had difficulty understanding the Creators, but also the reason I joined with Gelmir so many years ago.

One day I will meet the man who killed my family and destroyed my life.

I have been training for that day for years now. Skills that were honed over time and perfected with Gelmir's teaching had created a formidable Guardian out of me.

The day would come when I would meet Jericho, the tattooed Immortal of darkness, and on that day I would avenge my mother's death and kill him.

With my thoughts wandering far and wide over the past, I tried to relax and make myself comfortable in the overstuffed chair, just enough so I could sleep.

With my bones sinking into the cushioning of the chair, I readjusted and had almost dosed off, when the beautiful Dylan made a slight noise in her sleep. Directing my attention towards her, I watched as she shifted her body in an attempt to get more comfortable.

God, but she was beautiful. I thought so to myself earlier, when she had been on her bike and I had caught my first glimpse of her. She had almost hit me, and would have if I hadn't gotten my wits back before impact and jumped straight up, missing the bike. I was barely able to land steadily; she was that exceptional.

Feeling uncomfortable with the emotions that were heating my body heavily, I had stayed only long enough to see her turn around on the bike. One last look before moving out of site and around the house was all I dared take.

Gelmir and I were only on the reservation to gather as many Prime ancestors as we could find. We were to bring them back into the fold, educate them and prepare them for what was surely to come. Hopefully saving lives in the process.

I didn't need to attract unnecessary attention from a bike accident, nor a beautiful girl. Keeping a low profile was absolutely necessary. If the darkness and its followers ever found an Immortal before Gelmir and I were able to sequester them, they could be lost to us and bonded with evil. We couldn't afford many more losses to the

Darkness. So, getting a young girl interested in me was not an option at this point, and by the way she had stared at me, she was interested.

I know the effect I have on women. Easily swayed by my good looks, it had been a blessing in the past when I had been younger and had encouraged their behavior. Only as time passed had it become a curse. It was a curse I carried with me daily; a curse that changed my personality so much so that even if given the opportunity to get close, they wouldn't stay for long. Inevitably they had all wanted more from me. More was something I was not willing to give. Not now, not ever.

I had been down that road once before, and even if I did find a woman who could understand my nature, she would eventually die, leaving me alone once again.

No, I would never go down that road again. Time had shown me over and over that I needed distance from the female species. I took care of the basic needs, of course, but never with the same woman.

Each that I favored in my bed was handsomely paid for her efforts and then promptly left behind. I had convinced myself that it was the only way.

Over time, I stopped seeing mortal women altogether. I had met another Immortal, a woman named Sophia, and together we had shared the pleasures of an intimate relationship.

Sophia had been the one to lay the ground rules. Never would there be a relationship between us. She loved her freedom too much. It was the perfect arrangement. She enjoyed men of all cultures, shapes, and sizes;

and being tied down to a single Immortal man for eternity was not to her liking. It was the only arrangement I had ever thought would work.

Hearing a soft sigh, I looked back at the slumbering form lying on the sofa. Immediately I knew it was a mistake. I mentally stretched my mind to think of something else, but it was no use. It had been a long time since I had seen Sophia.

The sight of the light blue t-shirt straining over the swell of Dylan's breasts gave me the uncomfortable response I had been trying to avoid all evening.

With her unconscious movement, she had moved the top of her t-shirt down dangerously low, and it was taking every effort I had not to go over and wrap my arms around her and kiss the silly little pout from her dreaming lips.

I had been successful ignoring her presence for the most part, trying to forget the way she had looked at me after finally opening her eyes on the kitchen floor. She had devoured me, and it was literally driving me to distraction.

Standing, I paced the small living room. Emily had returned hours ago and, prior to retiring for the night, checked on both Dylan and Gelmir. Everyone was asleep with the exception of me. It wasn't looking too promising that the tightening grasping my maleness was planning on leaving anytime soon and so sleep would have to wait.

Alone, watching over her as Gelmir had wished, I tried to fight the battle warring in both my mind and body. She had sliced though my defenses and stole into my thoughts. No one had ever gotten as far as her, and that pissed me off.

Lust, mixed with anger, strengthened my pace. Walking with firm steps and long strides, I continued to fume. I had trained long and hard with Gelmir, becoming strong and formidable. No girl with amazing beauty and untrained talent was going to bring me to my knees. I had fought stronger battles than this and won. I would do the same here. I had too.

It was one of the ways that the dark side was capable of gaining control of an Immortal. If they could get into your mind, it was difficult to get them out. She had no idea what she had done to me, but if she ever learned to harness her abilities, she would be very dangerous.

Dylan murmured in her sleep and shifted once again, this time exposing more of her supple breast and strangling my will in the process.

Shoving a hand through my hair and closing my eyes, I tried to block the vision of my mouth on her firm, supple flesh, caressing soft, sensitive skin with my rough, worn hands, teasing, tempting, and urging her forward into bliss.

She had wanted me earlier; I had felt it. Remembering the look in her eyes had only created more strain in my already overheated body.

Walking to the back door and stepping out into the cold night air, I thought, *Yeah, she is dangerous all right; the darkness should be afraid. But it's me I am afraid for now.*

Twelve

Dylan

Beams of sunlight from the open curtains slid over my face, pushing away the last remnants of the night, their warm touch heating my skin and beckoning me to rise.

Opening my eyes, I knew immediately that I wasn't where I was supposed to be; this was not home. Taking a quick inventory of my surroundings, I realized I was at Mrs. T's. The slight panic I had felt when confronted with the unknown had dissipated. Relaxed at being familiar with my surroundings, I melted into the sofa and began the morning ritual of stretching. Purring like a big cat, I curled and uncurled my body, until I heard his voice.

"About time you got up." He walked past the sofa and out the front door. Frozen in mid-stretch at the sound of his voice, I watched as he didn't bother to look my way before leaving the house.

I waited until I was sure he was gone and not coming back before I whipped off the blanket that Mrs. T had covered me with and leaped from the sofa to go in search of her. Walking around the corner of the small barrier wall into the kitchen, the events of last night came rushing back.

Some memories were mine, some were his. The strange man had called him Alessar. They rushed through me like a movie on fast-forward, creating havoc on my senses. Feeling queasy, I grabbed for the wall to steady my balance.

Trying my best to keep my stomach from coming up and out of my body, I closed my eyes and felt for the comfortable spot in my mind I had used in the past when I was unsettled with feelings I could not control.

The pictures of his memories were more than disturbing, they were traumatic. One in particular; it was of a small child witnessing horrific events and of a monster that haunted his dreams. It was a man monster, tattooed heavily about the chest and arms, laughing at his attempt to save a woman from being harmed, only to be struck down and beaten.

Shivering at the memory I had inadvertently acquired, I pushed away from the wall in an attempt to make it to the kitchen.

I hadn't made it far before I felt a presence. Gelmir was in the room with me, and he placed a hand on my shoulder to guide me the rest of the way into the kitchen.

"Have a seat," he said, pulling the chair farther out so I could slide into it.

"It can be a little unsettling when you begin to use your powers for the first time. It seems that last night was somewhat of an initiation into your talents." Smiling, he took the seat next to mine and handed me a glass filled with orange juice.

Accepting the glass, I looked to him and wondered about this strange mystery man and if it was safe to trust him.

"It's only orange juice, Dylan. The sugar in it will help you to feel a little better." Smiling again, he stood and walked to the counter where a basket of blueberry muffins were waiting to be eaten. Plucking one from the basket, he turned and presented it to me. Grabbing it from his hand, I realized just how hungry I was. Pulling it apart, I shoved pieces into my mouth as if I was a starving animal. I felt strangely famished, as if I hadn't eaten in days.

"It's normal, you know, to be so hungry." He looked at me and then directly at the muffin I had almost completely devoured.

"When you are more familiar with the effects your powers have on your body, you will have more control over how to feed it." Standing, he walked to the basket and grabbed another muffin and began eating it himself.

With a mouthful of muffin, I studied him and asked, "Who are you? And don't give me your name, that I already know, Gelmir."

"I think"—he pulled the chair out on the opposite side of the table and sat down—"that you already know the answer to that question."

"I think that you are wrong," I replied, grabbing the glass and finishing off the last of the OJ before continuing on. "I haven't got a clue who you are except that you're some creepy old guy, playing mind tricks on me and God only knows who else."

"Well, I never took you for an idiot, Dylan, so it must be that you're a liar." Smiling, he stood and walked to the kitchen sink. Grabbing a glass from the drain board, he filled it.

"What? I am not a liar. I haven't got a clue who you are and what you're doing here; for that matter, I'm not sure why I'm here." Looking around the room, I pushed away from the table and stood.

"Do you feel better? Have the visions stopped?" Turning from the sink, he smiled again.

Realization came when I looked into his eyes and saw he was trying to make me forget what I had been going through just moments ago. He had called me a liar on purpose, effectively changing my focus and allowing me to get control. Anger had worked.

"What are you doing to me?" Now a little more frustrated than angry, I sat back down in the kitchen chair. "I don't understand; please, just answer my questions and tell me what all this is," I said, throwing my hands in the air and making a wide arch with my arms.

"Calm down, Dylan." He moved back to the table and sat on the opposite side. "Before we begin our discussion, I would like to wait for Emily's return; she is almost here and will be joining us shortly."

I studied him as he drank from the glass he had filled earlier at the kitchen sink with water.

The back door opened, and Emily walked through, just as he had said she would. I glanced at her and then back to him, staring as if he had just performed some magic trick and poof, she was there.

"Ah, Emily; right on time." He looked at the clock and then back to her. "You said you would be gone for ten minutes, and you were gone exactly that." He smiled that all-knowing smile that I was beginning to hate and hid behind his glass of water.

"Well, of course I'm back; I just ran to the store for milk." Holding the quart of milk up, she proceeded to walk to the refrigerator. Opening the fridge, she placed the milk on the top shelf and quickly closed the door. Turning to me, she placed her hand on my back and gently rubbed.

"How are you feeling this morning, my dear?" The concern in her voice was obvious.

"Fine; a little confused, but fine." Grabbing her hand as it moved over my shoulder, I patted it to assure her.

"Well, I worried about you all night." Moving to the side of the table, she sat down beside me. "I did go over and explain to Meda and Ezra that you would be spending the night here." Sighing, she continued, "I thought it only best, under the circumstances."

"Yes, about those circumstances; can you explain to me what exactly happened last night?" Pleading with my eyes, I looked to her for the answers. She would tell me what was happening to me and what these strange events were; that is, if she knew.

Over the years Mrs. T had been a huge part of my life growing up. Not only had she been my next-door neighbor, but a confidant when I fought with my siblings or a friend or when I was having a bad day.

Not many people understood the friendship that we had; but it was there nevertheless, and it had bloomed out of respect for each other and the truth.

Yes, I knew she would tell me the truth; I could rely on that for sure.

"Whatever you want to know, Dylan, is best asked of Gelmir." She gently laid her hand over mine and looked to Gelmir to explain. "He will have the answers you seek; I am only here to watch over and guide you all these years."

A lump formed in my throat and another dose of reality began to sink in. She had been placed here to watch over me. With both hands pressed flat on the kitchen table, I stretched my mind and relayed every encounter and memory I had had over the past twenty years with "Emily." Suddenly, he was there with me again, just as he was last night.

Snapping my head in his direction, I stared at him as he spoke to me without using words. "She was placed at your side to care for you and to make sure you were safe as you grew. Is that what you seek to learn from your memories, Dylan?"

Wiping my mind clear and focusing my anger directly at him, I screamed, "Get out of my head!"

"As you wish, Dylan." Turning, he spoke to Emily.

"Emily, would you be so kind as to retrieve my book from your spare bedroom?" He placed his hand over hers, and she silently rose to do his bidding.

We waited in silence, staring at each other. Not wanting him in my head again, I carefully thought of things that would be less than revealing if he should pop in.

Hearing the return of Mrs. T, I turned to see her place a large leather-bound book on the table in front of us. It looked to be older than any other book I had ever seen.

On a school trip to Washington, D.C., we had taken tours of the normal sights, including all the major monuments and several museums. At one of the museums we attended, there had been artifacts on display from centuries before. Within said artifacts were a few books; the book Gelmir now held in his hands and was gently opening had to have been just as old, if not older.

Turning back to me, he explained as he leafed through the pages, looking for the one that he needed.

"This, my dear Dylan," he explained with a nod toward the tome, "is the book of lineage, or, as some still calls it, the Book of Life." He continued to leaf though the pages. "It is the reference in which we"—glancing up from his perusal of the book to look at me—"meaning you and all other Immortals that we know of, are recorded."

The look on my face didn't detour him from continuing. "In this book we have recorded the birth and death of every Immortal who has ever graced this world." He paused before looking to me and added, "That is, if we are aware of their birth. There are those who have been lost to us, and of course, we have no way of knowing if they have procreated and where they are in this world."

A little dumbfounded at his words, I turned to Mrs. T with concern written all over my face. "He's lost his mind; the man is absolutely nuts! Does he have any idea what he is saying? There is no such thing as Immortals."

Watching as Emily—Mrs. T—looked from me to him and back again, she shrugged and only smiled as she said, "Dylan, it may sound farfetched to you now, but trust me, this is your history, and you would be wise to pay attention."

"Okay, fine, go ahead. Tell me how it is." A little angry at Emily's response and not sure why she would go along with his story, I turned my anger on him. "Tell me how you're an Immortal, how I'm an Immortal, and how the hell it is that no one has ever heard of any such creatures except for in sci-fi books and the movies?"

With the book now open to the page that he wanted, Gelmir turned the tome on the table so that the page in question could easily be seen. With one hand, he slid the book in front of me and placed a single finger on the second paragraph down.

It was a list of births for the year that I was born. Three names were present, and mine was the third line down. Beside the name Dylan Merrin Ella was the name of my parents. I placed both hands on the book and slid it closer, looking down at the printed names next to mine.

Dylan Merrin Ella—female child born on this day

July 14, 1985, in Dublin, Ireland, to mother: Isda
Ella of the Collective, father: unknown

Staring at the page in the book, a rollercoaster of emotion went through me. Isda was my mother's name. Who was she? Where was she? Was she alive? I could feel the tears welling up inside, and fearful that they would spill out; I turned the book and pushed it back to Gelmir.

"What is this? That is not me. I have parents; Ezra and Meda Black are my parents." Not sure I could stop the tears that were threatening to spill over, I moved to stand and leave, but Emily quickly clasped my hand and held me in place.

Settling back into my seat, I listened as she described the hardest days of her life.

"Twenty-two years ago, I brought a beautiful little girl to this reservation and gave her to the Black family to raise." Looking into her eyes, I could see the concern she held there and wondered if the tears that threatened to cloud my vision were from the pain I was feeling or a response to the pain I could see in her eyes.

Blinking hard to keep the tears at bay, I could clearly see the agony the memories were causing her; yet I needed to be sure, so I probed, making sure if what I was seeing, she was truly feeling.

She continued, and I got nothing but the feeling of pure honesty from her. "I had to leave you with them in order to keep you safe; it was thirty-one months later before I was able to get back to you." Sighing as she reached for my hand, I pulled it from her grasp.

"You have no idea how hard it was to hide you. Your mother had entrusted your safety to me, and the only thing that I could do was abandon you with strangers in order to make sure you were safe." Turning to Gelmir for support, he held her hand and she continued on.

"At the time, it was the only option I had left." Looking to me as she continued, she said, "We—your mother, you, and I—had just left our homelands in the hopes of avoiding the upcoming battles that were progressing toward us. Abaddon had discovered that a key had been hidden somewhere in the highlands, and the battle for ownership had been going for some time."

I watched as Gelmir rubbed a scar on his hand and then silently willed Emily to continue.

"We were traveling mostly at night and avoiding all Immortals, trying to get you out of the country and somewhere safe when the Dark Lord Abaddon found us and set his minions upon us." Pausing in her explanation, she grabbed the glass of water Gelmir had placed in front of her and gulped down the last of it, before proceeding.

"Isda is a Collector; she knew the only way that we were going to survive was if she, being the much stronger Immortal, battled the darkness alone, buying time for you and me to escape. I didn't agree with her; I felt I could help or that if we all ran we could surely outwit them and get away. But she had insisted. She didn't want to take a chance with your safety. She placed you in my arms and begged me to go."

She wept, tears streamed down her face at the painful memories of that day. I could feel the pain she was going though and from somewhere deep inside, I knew she had regretted her decision to leave my mother behind. Wiping her tears and gathering her strength, she went on.

"Without help from the family, I had nowhere to turn. I cut your hair, put you in boy's clothes, and disguised myself as you see me now." Looking to make sure that I was still listening and seeing confirmation in what I saw, she continued.

"We managed to lose the Dark Lords in our travels, but I knew they would never stop looking for you. In order to make sure you would never be found, I went back." Looking directly in my eyes, I could see she was now afraid of how I would feel with the information she was about to reveal.

"I went back with the intention of making anyone who cared about you think you were dead." She looked to Gelmir for support; seeing that he was still with her, she continued on.

"With Gelmir's help, we convinced the Dark Lord you had been lost to us all in battle." Sighing at the memories of the past, she went on, "No one knows of your existence with the exception of myself, Gelmir, and now Alessar. It was the only way we could make sure you were safe."

Staring at the woman I thought I knew for so many years, I drew a blank as to what I should say to her. So many questions were running through my mind; I didn't know where to begin. If my real mother had given me to her, why was it that she did not know of my existence now? Where was she? Why wasn't she here? Confused and wanting answers but afraid of what I might hear, I started with the one that popped into my head first and seemed harmless.

"As I see you now?" The question came out as a whisper on my breath. Gaining courage and looking directly at Emily, I asked the question again firmly. "You said, as I see you now. We were on the run from the Dark Lord, and you changed my appearance to that of a boy. You did the same so you looked as you do now; that is what you said. What did you mean by that?"

She looked to Gelmir as if to determine if she should proceed. Finding the support she needed, she continued "What I meant by that, is this." Pushing back from the table, she stood and moved to the end of the kitchen.

The air shifted in the room and suddenly light came from every inch of her body. At first I blinked my eyes against the strong glow she was creating, but began eventually blinking them because I couldn't believe what I was seeing. She had transformed. Closing and opening my eyes again and again did not change the affect of what I was seeing.

When I opened them for the final time, I was astounded at what I saw standing before me. Where there had been a worn, old Native American woman just moments ago, now there stood a young, beautiful woman with hair the color of winter wheat past her waist, and a thin waist at that.

She was completely transformed, looking nothing like the woman I had grown up knowing, until I looked into her eyes. The same dark, chocolate brown eyes that had looked so lovingly at me over the years were now watching me intently for my response.

She stepped forward, and I jumped from my seat. Standing, I began to stutter my words, not sure what to think or say.

She froze in mid-step and reached out her hand. "It's okay, Dylan. This is who I am; the person you are familiar with is just a cloak I created when I needed to make sure that we were safe from the Dark Lords." Stepping forward, she placed her hand in mine and entwined our fingers, something we used to do when I was younger and she was taking care of me. Looking at our hands, she went on.

"You are not the only one who has sacrificed for the well-being of our people. Many have given their entire lives in the hopes that one day an end will be near." Turning her eyes to Gelmir for acknowledgement and support before continuing, she said "It seems that the end is almost upon us now and my job of protecting you is no longer required."

Turning back to me, she finished, "I will return home and help my friends and family in the fight against the darkness, where hopefully we will succeed. Then you, young Dylan, will never have to see the ravages made by darkness and its strength in this world."

After giving me a brief hug, she walked to Gelmir and took his hand. "Finish telling her, Gelmir; she needs to hear it all." Smiling back at me, she let go of Gelmir's hand and stepped away.

"Please understand, Dylan, everything I did was for your safety. Your mother was my best friend, and at the time, I could see no other way." Turning toward the door leading outside, I watched as she stepped gracefully over the threshold and glanced back one last time before leaving the small dwelling.

Now alone with Gelmir, I became increasingly aware of him watching me; instead of probing his mind and getting more than I bargained for, like finding him inside of my head, I opted for the path of least resistance and just asked for the answers that I wanted.

"So, you heard her; spill it. I want to know it all." Putting on my oh-so-tough exterior so that I wouldn't break down and cry like I wanted to, I moved from the small kitchen and walked into the living room and sat down on the sofa I had just risen from not but an hour ago.

He followed my lead and walked into the living room behind me. As if he wasn't sure whether or not I planned to bolt, he stood in front of the living room door, as if barring my exit.

What he didn't know was that I didn't plan on going anywhere. I needed the answers that Emily felt I was owed. I had been searching for them for some time, and she knew it. I always knew that I was different and thought it was because there was something wrong with me.

God, I was pissed off. She had known all along and never said anything. Why? How many times had she found me crying because someone had been hateful to the strange little blonde girl? How many fights could have been avoided had she just been honest with me? My mind was racing and my anger was building.

I had never felt completely whole, as if I didn't belong in this world, never knowing or even contemplating that it would be something as extreme as immortality. I was somebody, not just the crazy blonde girl from the reservation that no one liked because she was different or strange. There were answers to my questions, and the man who had them was now sitting in front of me, looking rather distraught over the outcome of this morning's events.

No, I wasn't going anywhere. Not with the answers that I needed about to be given. Good or bad, I needed to understand who I was.

Thirteen

Alessar

The screen door slammed behind me as I stomped across a lawn of dry grass. The heat of the summer and the lack of water had turned its spring green lushness quite brown. Propelled by the powerful emotions brewing inside me, I walked to the sidewalk and stood. Turning east towards the edge of town, I began running. Slowly at first, unsure as to where I was going, knowing only that I needed to get away. Away from the thoughts that plagued my mind.

The day had just begun and it was exceptionally hot already. I didn't care—the hotter the better. With sweat rolling down my face, its saltiness stinging my eyes, I pushed my body even harder. I would run and train, working out some of the feelings that had been troubling me recently.

Pushing myself to move faster, I felt my body react. Immortal blood was pumping through my veins. My limbs were filled with the essence of life and youth, giving me the awesome sensation of being indestructible, an emotion that was so familiar to me when I would run.

While running past the town buildings, I was careful to control my speed. Life in this small town of Mission was beginning to stir. Wives were sending their husbands off to work with a goodbye kiss. Store owners were unlocking their establishments and preparing for the day's business.

Struck by a strange feeling of envy, I watched as the daily morning routine of several residents played out before me. My mind began to wonder, taking me back to the days of my childhood. The days before the darkness had consumed my world. Memories of my mother, her beautiful smile, the softness of her hair and the happiness that we shared together. The memory of her touch, as she would stroke my forehead while singing me to sleep. I missed her.

Wrapped in the past and increasing my speed, I had almost forgotten about the beauty back at the house. Almost was an understatement, a lie really. She was always there. Hidden in the recesses of my mind was the scent of her skin, the blue of her eyes and the curve of her hips. God, she was like an itch that could never be scratched.

Endeavoring to shake off the persistent itch that was now Dylan, I ran faster. With thoughts of her riding shotgun over my mind, I pushed my body harder. I needed to forget. Yet my mind wanted to retrace every word and thought I ever had about her. If I couldn't evict her from my head, then I would run my body to exhaustion. Running faster still, attempting to forget, and knowing that it would never happen.

I had been exceptionally rude to the slow-waking beauty on the sofa this morning and the guilt of that action was eating me up inside. I could have kicked myself for letting any emotions like that show. Weakness was not something a Guardian could afford, not this late in the fight against darkness. No Guardian could afford to have such distractions.

I just needed to push her from my mind and work hard at training today. There was no time for anything more.

Slowing my stride, I took in the surroundings. I had made it to the end of town and was determining which way to go. To the left was a simple dirt road that led straight out to the highway and then to the interstate that divided the state in half. In the opposite direction to the right were rolling hills, rough terrain and the stark beauty of the Badlands. Deciding on the path that would give me the most challenging and vigorous workout, I turned to the right. With the Badlands and its beautiful terrain in front of me, I raced forward.

Trying to wipe my mind clear, I gave myself over to the workout, offering my body what it needed and letting my brain attempt to forget her. Yet no matter what I did, I seemed to draw her back to me again and again. I had only been around her for a short period of time, but she was there always. She was in my head. Working on my mind in ways that she had no clue she possessed.

That's what bothered me the most—she had gotten too close. She had seen me from the inside and out. With no control over her doing so, I had hopelessly been lost. I understood that it had been an accident when she entered my body as an immortal collector. Even so, what she had done connected us together. It affected me in ways I didn't understand and if I had any say in the matter, she would never gain that knowledge.

Pushing myself harder, I sprinted toward my new destination, a bluff covered in trees and shrubs about ten miles ahead of me. Running with the wind at my back, I was literally flying across the country. With the Badlands all around me, I concentrated on the power that was pumping though my body. Gaining more speed, I was eating up the ground, moving faster than ever before. A sensation of extreme power entered my body. I could feel more force with each step I took. An energy that I had never felt before raced through my body and filled me with a drive that overtook me completely.

Unfamiliar with this new power, I slowed my run. Shaking with the force of its strength I tried to understand where it had come from. Unable to completely understand, I conceded. It would need to wait until I could speak with Gelmir. It wasn't the first time that I had experienced a new gift and it would not be the last.

Taking in the surroundings, I thought about how beautiful the landscape was as I ran. I cataloged every detail with my eyes. It was beautiful from the layers of color etched into the terrain of the Badlands, to the pasture ground where cattle roamed freely, grazing the countryside. In the distance, the Black Hills rose onto the horizon. It was a remarkable sight. This country was truly majestic, with views of the rolling plains and the beautiful mountains; it was understandable why Emily called it her Old West.

Running hard and fast, I covered miles of ground before stopping to take a breath. Focusing on gifts of an Immortal, I trained, making sure I would be ready for the battles that would surely come, now that the Chosen One was among us. I would need to be prepared in a moment's notice.

I needed to be stronger. My body is strong. I have strength unknown to man and my ability to run faster than most animals and Immortals alike has always given me the edge against my enemies, and yet my mind was still in training.

Gelmir had begun my tutoring when we had first met many years ago. Immortals were gifted with several abilities. Some of which came naturally, and others that needed to be nurtured and trained over time. This allowed an Immortal to utilize nurtured gifts and make them much more effective during battle.

I have always been able to do battle of the physical nature with little or no resistance from my opponents. As a Guardian, I was gifted with exceptional strength and speed, that of a true warrior. For the Prime, I am a strong champion. Against the evil of darkness I pose a great threat. However, before Gelmir took me under his wing and began his training in the art of mind control, the odds were not always in my favor. I had to be careful when battling an Immortal with gifts of the mind. It didn't matter if I had strength in abundance within my body. If the immortal I was battling could achieve control of my psyche, I could possibly lose my life.

Gelmir was training me on how to control my thoughts. To guard against Immortals who had the strength to change the reality of their victims. Controlling one's own perception of reality and not allowing another Immortal to enter the mind was difficult. I was capable against an untrained and the lesser-talented Immortals, but any who were gifted at birth and wielded its power was a different story.

They could change the truth for their own self-ish needs, using their victims to do their bidding. If an Immortal wanted control, he or she would mind bend the subject, rendering them completely oblivious to their own will. The lives of weaker immortals were being manipulated, by the darkness. Their bodies and souls were devoured, making them all too aware of their actions and the unwilling deeds they were committing. They were turned into simple puppets, with the controlling Immortal pulling all the strings. Falling victim to the darkness and effectively becoming both the predator and the prey. Unable to stop them, it was cruelty in the worse way. Cringing at the thought, I pressed myself to train harder. I would never be lost to the darkness that way. No matter what it took, I would not do the bidding of evil.

Any Immortal who was capable of such actions was doing so for the dark side. It meant one of two things: either they deemed their prey worthy of their goal and could eventually use them for their own selfish needs, or they posed too much of a threat and were not desired by the Dark Lords as minions.

If the Dark Lords found them unworthy, elimination was the only option given. Death was usually the end result for most Immortals who were unwilling to submit. It was easier than taking the time to mind bend them. Yet there were those who took sick pleasure in treating them so. Like a mouse being toyed with by a cat, they would play with their prey.

Mind bending was the ultimate demise for any Immortal. It was the fear of being unable to defend yourself, no longer capable of controlling your own thoughts and thrown into the depths of despair. Most who were turned to the darkness unwillingly prayed for death before they completely lost their souls.

That fear was what made the Immortals so fearsome in battle. They had nothing to lose by dying.

With so much to still learn, I trained, pushing myself to the limit. With my mind I created the tools that I needed to protect myself. I worked hard and I had proven my strength in many ways; but in the past few days, I had been tricked and probed, intentionally and not so intentionally, by two different women. Both had pissed me off.

Golda had been looking to eliminate me and had almost succeeded in her task. If it had not been for Gelmir, I may have walked off the edge of the cliff, seriously maiming myself on the rocks below. Weak and unprotected, her dark travelers could come in and finish me off.

The young Immortal, Dylan, had probed my thoughts as well. She had gained access with little or no difficulty. She meant no harm; in fact, I was pretty sure that she didn't even know the extent of her own powers. Somehow she had slipped into my mind, past most of my defenses and had explored my brain. She had done it so quickly that I had little time to throw up the protective walls to block her and keep her from getting too deep.

I knew exactly when she had gotten in, and I was at a loss on how to stop her. Each time I built a barrier; she would knock it down or find a way to get around it, even before I had completed its construction. If Gelmir hadn't assisted me, she could have completely stripped down my defensives, taking what she wanted and leaving nothing of me behind. Only a shell of the man I was would exist.

My abilities were completely known to her. They were spread out on a table, as if they were a buffet on display for her consumption. She now contained the knowledge to destroy me. It wouldn't take long to do so, should she ever feel the need and gain control of her gifts. With all my knowledge and strength at her will, it left nothing to the imagination.

Unsettled by that thought, I pushed my mind further. Strengthening it for battle, making sure that I would be prepared the next time an attempt was made. Giving her easy access into my mind was not going to happen again. She was strong, but she had no knowledge of how to wield her powers. She didn't understand the strength she possessed. Yet, I was not completely sure of victory when battling against her the next time.

She knew the intimate details of my life. She knew my likes and dislikes, my strengths and weaknesses. She had the ability to control me in ways that scared even my hardened Warrior heart. Feeling a little sickened at the thought of someone having so much of me, I stopped and bent over with queasiness. She had not just read my mind, but rather had absorbed my very essence, leaving me weak and vulnerable. With intimate knowledge of my capabilities, I felt something that I hadn't felt in a very long time. I was scared, and that was just unacceptable.

Feeling stripped and afraid of the power she unwittingly held, not just over me, but any Immortal who was captured by her lure, I willed myself to train harder.

Standing tall and strong, I pushed back the threat that Dylan posed to me, and I tapped into my senses. Using my mind, I worked at improving my skills and utilized the training Gelmir had shown me, not so long ago. He had given me tools to help cultivate my mind and grow strength in order to protect myself, as well as those I have sworn to protect. Digging deep within myself, I pulled a large breath of air into my lungs and felt the surge of power expand through my body, feeding my intellect and strengthening my gift.

I would need to improve my potency of mind if I planned to continue with Gelmir and the quest to stop the darkness. Since meeting the young Immortal Dylan and learning of her strength, it was now more important than ever. She was stronger than any Immortal I had ever seen, and her abilities were in their infant stages.

Trust was what I had to focus on. I had to trust in Gelmir. Together now for some time, I had never doubted the reasoning for the things Gelmir did. There had always been a motive to his actions. Sometimes they were not obvious, but eventually they became known.

This was no different. Gelmir had reasons for keeping Dylan hidden for so long and not taking her into training sooner. The question was, what were they?

If she had fallen into the wrong hands and been influenced by the darkness, Lord only knows how much damage she could have inflicted. I could only imagine just how bad life on this planet would have been.

No, there was a reason for Gelmir's actions. This young Immortal was special, I knew that. She had been secreted away with no one but Gelmir and Emily knowing of her whereabouts. Not even her mother had known where she was or even that she was still alive. Isda must have been heartbroken to see her only daughter taken from her, never knowing what became of her.

I couldn't think of a reason strong enough that would keep me from being with my family, if I had one. Not even the threat of death would keep me away. I have wished my entire life that my mother was with me. The pain I felt at her death was horrific, but the pain Isda must have gone through would have been unbearable. No, I wouldn't have done that to myself or my child.

I would have to trust Gelmir and understand that whatever possessed him to hide her was beyond question. I knew Gelmir would tell me eventually, and if not Gelmir, then Emily would.

When Gelmir had explained we were going to meet with Emily to see about an Immortal she had been watching over, I had been curious. Questioning him about the mysterious Immortal had gotten me nowhere. So with Gelmir unwilling to give up more information, I drew on my past memories of Emily.

I didn't know much about her. I had met her some time ago with Gelmir and had discovered that she was a talented Immortal, able to speak to the animals and manipulate the elements. She was what they called an Elementor of nature. Moving wind and water with just a thought, transforming the land and plant life at will and when necessary, she could cloak or shape shift. She was a strong Immortal, and she was kind in every sense of the word.

It had been Emily who had shown me the basics on speaking with the animals. Not that I was really good at it, but I could get the animals to understand to some degree, as well as understand some of what they communicated back. It was very handy when I was in unfamiliar territory. They could lead me to water and food if necessary, and warn me of danger. They also made for great companionship if ever I found myself alone and in need of company.

At the moment, I felt like some friendly animal company would do me good. Continuing with my training, and taking a much-needed break from the problem at hand, I sat down on the edge of a small gray boulder. Reaching out with my mind and sharpening my hearing, I searched the Badlands and prairies.

I could hear several creatures roaming the country. Prairie dog families were chatting in the distance, their barking heard easily. They were talking to each other from one den to the next.

The sounds of several prairie animals, both large and small, penetrated my skull. Creatures that sheltered in and around the Badlands could be heard going about their daily routine. The white tail deer and antelope were grazing. The fox and the coyote were searching for their next meal and the hum of other animals cascaded though my mind. The land was teeming with wildlife.

The coyote was one of my favorite animals. They were scavengers at heart, but it was their unwavering determination and the fact that they were very curious animals that gave them the fondness that I carried. Coyotes were easily tempted by their curiosity, and I was one to use that to my favor.

Cupping my hands around my mouth, I barked. Calling to one coyote that was not far away, I requested some company. It was only a matter of time to see if my request would be granted. Communicating to the animals didn't always work. In fact, most of the time my attempts to do so failed. However, every now and then, I would succeed in getting an animal to join me for a brief conversation.

The coyote had heard my call, and responded with a yip and bark that I didn't fully understand. Again I cupped my hands and barked back in response wanting desperately to understand and speak to the wild animal. With the coyote responding a second time, I knew his curiosity had gotten the better him. I could hear as the coyote approach with my sharpened senses. Digging into my pocket, I pulled out some jerky I had swiped earlier from Emily's kitchen and waited for my guest to arrive.

I watched as the coyote slowly crept toward me. Unsure of what to expect, the coyote danced back and forth, preparing for a quick exit if necessary. One step forward, then one step back, stepping from side to side, dancing, and becoming more nervous by the moment.

Reaching into his mind, I spoke softly. Taking the jerky, I threw it on the ground and watched as the coyote stopped his dancing and directed his attention toward it.

Extending his silver gray head forward, he sniffed the air and walked toward the salted treat. With the smell of jerky lying on the ground where it had been thrown, he stepped even closer.

Taking pity on him, I reached out with my mind again and spoke to the animal. "It is all right. I will not hurt you."

Standing still, the animal directed his eyes first to me sitting on the boulder, and then to the jerky laying at his feet.

Stepping forward, he yipped at me, stepped to where the jerky lay on the ground and began sniffing. First the air, then the ground before proceeding to devour the meat. When he was finished, he stood still and looked to me again. I had spoken to him and he was curious. Curious enough, that he took another step forward, touching my hand with one swipe of his snout.

"Well, hello. I didn't know if you were going to be friendly or not, but glad to see that you are." I spoke to the animal with kindness and stroked the fur on the back of his neck. "Would you like to have another little bit of jerky? I believe I have one more piece in my pocket." Grabbing the second piece from my sweat pants pocket, I extended my hand and watched as the beautiful creature ate it from my palm.

Stroking the fur slowly, I spoke to the coyote and wondered just how much he could understand.

"You know, you have it pretty good right now. I am actually finding myself a little jealous of the fact that you have a full stomach and are getting such a nice massage." I continued to rub the back of the coyote's neck, moving over his shoulders and down his spine. He was a beautiful creature.

Not a very large animal, the coyote was no bigger than the average-sized dog. His speckled gray and brown coat was thick and healthy. He looked to be in good shape, with wonderful muscle tone and a great sense of strength, he was a formidable animal. He wasn't very old, probably one of the younger males in the pack. Definitely not the alpha dog, but he had the potential of a warrior and his pack would benefit from that.

We sat there together for some time, continuing our conversation and relaxing in each other's company. I was at ease, something that I hadn't felt in a very long time.

Suddenly the coyote stood, perking his ears toward the sky; he became completely aware of his surrounding and on full alert. With a sharp yip, he moved toward the tall grass. He gave a final look behind him, followed by a second yip, and he was gone. In a full run, he sprinted forward, going in the same direction from which he had come.

Alert now myself, I listened and could hear nothing in the near vicinity; it was silent all around.

There was silence where there had once been life. Nature's liveliness was gone. The sound of animals scurrying about, moving from here to there doing their normal daily activities had ceased. No prairie dogs, with their constant barking, could be heard. It was as if the entire Badlands and prairie had fallen under some spell of silence, sucked dry of life and left completely void.

Reaching farther out with my senses, I felt them before I heard them. Immortals! And they were not the average young bloods. These Immortals had power. I could feel their strength exuding from them and shivered as its evil essence came me. With wickedness all about them it was obvious to me and to the animals residing here, that they came from darkness of the worst kind.

Stretching my senses even farther out, I could see that they were traveling fast. There were three of them-two men and a woman. I sensed the brawn within the men, but it was the woman who was shrouded in darkness and power that made me nervous. Trying to get a better feel for her, I pressed again.

She sensed me immediately. I had opened my mind to see who they were, tapping into the men easily and finding that they were no great threat. She, on the other hand, had been difficult. No sooner had I looked to her than I found myself falling backwards onto my ass. A surge of pain shot through my head, and a voice came to me on the air, "We are coming, Alessar." The voice rendered me completely still and utterly unnerved. Who the hell was she, and how did she know my name?

Jumping to my feet, I sprinted toward town. I raced to reach Gelmir, Emily, and the beautiful Dylan, before the evil who was coming full speed ahead, reached them.

Fourteen

Dylan

"Okay, I'm listening; spill it all and give me the answers I have been waiting for." I slumped against the side of the sofa, trying to gather my strength.

It had been a rather disturbing morning, not to mention the evening before. Finding out that you were different wasn't so bad, because somewhere deep down inside you already knew that. But finding out you were Immortal and you were hidden away from any family that you may have had for your own protection, was harder to swallow.

"So what did Mrs. T, I mean Emily, what did she mean by protecting me from the darkness, and where is my mother?" It was hard to believe that just a few moments ago the woman who had always been known as an older, motherly type had transformed before my very eyes and was really a much younger looking and very beautiful Immortal woman.

Carefully watching him, examining every move he made, I waited for the answer that would come and prepared for what he would say. Was he going to tell the truth? I needed to be ready, sharpening my senses to make sure he was being truthful and not placating me with half-truths to keep my curiosity at bay. That just wouldn't work today.

Shifting in his seat, he looked uncomfortable, almost as if he was trying to sense just how much he should say, before saying anything at all.

When his inner battle was won, he spoke, "What she was referring to is the darkness that surrounds our kind and wishes to enslave us for eternity." He spoke directly, and with every sense that I had available, without having to reach into his mind where I didn't want to be, I searched and felt no inkling of deceit. Disappointed with his answer, I questioned him farther.

"Okey dokey, then…" I said a little sarcastically. I pressed for more. "I'm not sure exactly how I fit into this picture, but do you think you could elaborate a little more and give something like, oh, I don't know, details." I was pissed and rightly so; he had been direct but vague as well, and he knew it.

Piercing him with my eyes, I mentally dared him too be vague again, watching as he deliberated with himself on just how much information he should divulge.

He wasn't trying to hide anything; it was obvious that he wished to tell me all, but something was stopping him from doing so. Frustrated at waiting for answers, I took a chance and probed his mind, looking for the answers on my own.

He was there again, just as he had been the night before, waiting for the moment when our minds united and we could speak to each other in private.

He spoke, "Thank you for reaching out, Dylan; I knew if I was patient you would eventually come for the answers you seek." Looking into his eyes of crystal blue, their depths held concern—concern for me.

"I wish I could tell you everything that you want to know, but there are some things you must find out for yourself. I will do my best to fill in the blanks, but it is up to you to find the answers you seek." Shifting in his seat, he adjusted the brown tunic he wore today. Digging into its pocket, he pulled out a necklace.

"This belongs to you." Extending his hand, he placed the necklace on the small end table next to the sofa. "Your mother gave it to you when you were a very young girl."

Staring at the delicate necklace he had just laid down, I was mesmerized by it. He continued speaking. "Before you left with Emily for your own safety, Isda gave it to you. It belonged to her, and she wanted to make sure you always had a piece of her with you."

Reaching for the delicate piece of jewelry, slowly running my hand over the cool chain, a surge of power coursed up and though my fingers.

"There wasn't a single day that I didn't see her wearing it. I believe that a very special person to your mother gave it to her. She never removed it until she gave it to you."

Picking up the chain and holding it between shaking fingers, I could see the beauty of the crystal lying in the palm of my hand.

Another jolt of energy burst though my body, but this time images of the past came with it. They were memories of a time when I was happy, memories of a young woman and man standing together, holding hands. They were smiling and very happy.

The image was fleeting, there one minute and gone the next. Needing more, I clenched the necklace in my hand; holding it tightly to my chest, I closed my eyes and concentrated on what I had just seen. Nothing. It was gone. Trying one more time, I squeezed tighter to the necklace, and again nothing came.

Opening my eyes, I could see the reflection of my despair in Gelmir's eyes. Feeling the burn of tears beginning to well, I turned so that he could not see my anguish. I couldn't afford to be weak right now; the answers I had been searching for were here for the taking. Pushing back the tears and clearing my throat, I turned back and grilled him for answers.

"Why, then, did you have it and I didn't?" I asked, taking my frustration out on him.

"I only took it so that it would not be lost." He sighed, realizing that details were necessary for his explanation, so he went on, "When Emily brought you here to this place, it was under the assumption that it wouldn't be permanent. She needed a place to hide you." Taking a deep breath, he stood and walked to the sofa. Sitting down, he placed his hand on top of mine and continued,

"Somewhere safe, with someone who could watch over you and protect you until she was able to come back for you."

"I don't understand. Who, exactly, was she protecting me from?" Looking into his eyes, he spoke again, but this time it was with only his mind.

"Hold my hand, Dylan. Listen to my thoughts. You will see for yourself through my memories and those of your ancestors."

Grasping his hand tightly, determination rolled through my body. I shifted to a more comfortable position and replied, "I'm ready when you are."

"Understand, Dylan, what you are going to see may be confusing at first, but all will fall into place if you open your mind and listen for the answers." With both my hands firmly in his grip, he proceeded, "Relax, take a deep breath, and just let your mind do the rest. Open up, Dylan, and you will see all."

Leaning forward, stretching my back, and rolling my shoulders, I found a place of relaxation and said again, "Okay, I'm ready."

"All right, I want you to reach out with your mind and read my thoughts."

Shaking my head, I explained, "I tried that earlier, and it didn't really work for me; not so comfortable, if you get my meaning."

"I know, Dylan. That's because I wasn't guiding you. I will be there this time, and just so that you know, I will not let you see all, not until I feel you are ready."

Nodding my head, I straightened in my seat and used my mind, probing his. It wasn't easy; there was so much to decipher, images of people and places rapidly running though, one after the other.

"Concentrate, Dylan. You are getting an open book of information right now. These are the memories I have of your early life, before you came to live here."

Closing parts of my mind and opening others, I began to compartmentalize each picture, memory, and thought. Slowly at first, then faster, absorbing every detail Gelmir was giving, and reaching in for more.

"Slow down, Dylan. You are pushing too hard, and you're not ready yet."

I was ready. I needed the answers, and they were coming faster now. Thoughts, images, and information that was confusing and a little scary. I was devouring them, one after another, storing his memories as if they were my own.

Then it hit me—the pain was horrible! I screamed, releasing his hands and clutching my head. I slammed shut the doors that had been open and waited for the throbbing that permeated my entire head to dissipate. Gaining some control, I glanced in his direction. "Why did you do that? I was just getting the answers I needed."

"No, you were not, Dylan. You were taking what was not yours to take. I tried to warn you, and you didn't listen. You gave me no other choice."

Looking up at him and taking in his appearance, it was noticeable that he too had been in pain; he was still feeling some effect of it now. "What happened? What did I do?" Concerned with his appearance and worried that he was still hurting, I touched his hands.

"It was nothing that you could have stopped without help and training." He reached out and grabbed both my hands again, and with his mind, he said, "It's okay, Dylan. You will learn over time how to control your strength, and I will help you, but you must listen to me when I tell you what to do."

Holding his now fragile-looking hands between my own, I nodded in agreement. He looked so much older than he had before. It had only been a short time since I had met him, and yet I knew him better now than I did Mack. He needed rest. I had gotten enough information from him for now and knowing that I needed to be with him to understand who and what I was, I could wait for the rest.

We had come far, sitting on the sofa together, relaxing, and speaking of the images that had been pulled from his mind earlier. Time had given him some of the strength back that he had lost from our encounter together.

The same man who had scared me just the night before with his strange abilities was now seated beside me, speaking of the past as if we had been friends forever. We spoke of what the images meant to me and to him, reminiscing of the past, and teaching me about the future that was sure to come.

Sitting quietly, I listened to every word that rolled out of his mouth, absorbing them as if they were my lifeline to a reality I had never known. A knowledge and reality that had been hidden from me was now becoming quickly the only way I would understand a future that was coming into play.

None of it made sense; but then again, when was life sensible? I had been taught at a very young age that life wasn't fair and that it would never be easy, but I had no idea how difficult it would be until Alessar rushed through the door.

Fifteen

Alessar

Moving faster than ever before, I made good time back to the small house Emily had resided in for so many years. Bursting though the whitewashed screen door, I came to a stop before Gelmir and the young beauty, Dylan.

"Gelmir, we have to go. Now!" Glancing at the sofa where they sat and willing the young girl to not put up a fight, I raced past and into the spare bedroom, grabbing the few belongings we had brought with us. It was only after noticing that Gelmir was moving rather slowly that I took stock in his appearance.

He was weak, almost as if he had been in battle and drained of all energy, incapable of even standing. It was visible; Gelmir had been attacked, but by whom? Turning to the young woman who now stood beside the weakened man, I scowled and trained all my anger on her.

"What the hell have you done?" I addressed Dylan, moving toward the weakened Gelmir and grasping him by the arm.

"Alessar, stop it; we don't have much time. They will be here shortly, and we need to get to Mack's so he can travel us out of here. I don't have enough strength left to do it myself." Turning toward Dylan, Gelmir extended his hand and willed her to embrace it. "Much will be explained, but I fear that now is not the time. Do you trust me, Dylan?"

I watched as she searched her thoughts and feelings. I could see the turmoil she was in. She had no idea if she should trust this man. Gelmir had only recently been introduced to her, and it took time to earn trust.

What I did know was that if she wanted answers, she didn't have many alternatives. The answers to the questions she sought were within Gelmir. I watched as she placed her hand in his, and willing went with him. She would have to trust him to some extent. What she wanted and needed were locked inside of Gelmir, and the only way to them was through the trust he asked of her.

Glancing at the now entwined hands of the young beauty and Gelmir, I scowled and said, "Well, isn't that nice? Now, if you don't mind, Gelmir, I would like to get the hell out of here, before whoever the hell tapped into my thoughts catches up with us!" I attempted to propel the couple out the door.

Gelmir stopped dead in his tracks. I could see he was summoning strength from deep within himself. I had seen just that exact same will be harnessed during times of battle. Gelmir was strong and his mind was capable of going great lengths to defeat evil. I watched as he silently stood in place. Gelmir's eyes were closed and his face was strained with the effort that he was expelling to gain whatever knowledge he sought.

Time seemed to fly by, waiting for Gelmir to finish his mental surfing. It was ticking away. Every second of escape we had left was becoming more precious. I knew what it was that Gelmir sought. I had tried to find it myself and knew better than to attempt battling an immortal that strong. I had gotten away in time and knew the only hope that we had now with Gelmir so weak was to run. Touching Gelmir's shoulder and pressing the fact that we had little time left and we were wasting it standing here. His eyes flashed open. His entire face turned ghostly white before his knees buckled underneath him and he fell to the floor in front of the back door.

Emily rushed in and dropped beside him.

"Gelmir, what is it?" Holding his face between her hands, she pleaded with him to answer her, "Gelmir, please, answer me."

"It is Golda! She is with two seekers, and they hunt for her." His eyes moved from Emily to Dylan. The strained look he gave me was visible in his eyes, declaring the urgency with which they needed to move. Time was of the essence; they needed to hurry, and Gelmir was too weak to follow. I looked to Emily, willing her to understand. The look on her face said more than anything: that she knew exactly what she needed to do and she was scared.

Sacrifices were sometimes necessary if the Prime were to win battles against evil, and today would be no different. The only hope they had was to find the Chosen One, and that meant that it was crucial that Dylan survive. She could never be allowed to be taken over to the dark side.

I watched as Emily rose to her feet and stepped around the fallen Gelmir. Grabbing onto my arm, she pulled me aside, "You must go; they will be here shortly. Gelmir and I will protect you for as long as we can."

Reaching around her neck, she unclasped the chain that held a ring of pure gold securely to her bosom. With ring in hand, she glanced at both myself and Dylan before moving around the small home with stealth speed grabbing items and placing them in a backpack. Throwing the now full backpack to me, she moved to Dylan's side and slowly slid the golden ring onto her bare finger.

Holding Dylan's adorned hand in her own, she looked into her eyes and sighed. "This is my gift to you, Dylan. I had hoped I would be able to give this to you at a different time. At a time that would have allowed me to show you its treasures at length."

Smiling, she continued, "Understand that what you have in this ring is a tool. Use it wisely, my sweet girl." Placing her hand across Dylan's forehead, she gave her the knowledge and wisdom she needed in order to use the ring. "Be careful and move quickly."

Smiling once again, she began to move away, but stopped when she felt Dylan's reaction to the information she had just been given. "Yes, Dylan; you now have the abilities I was blessed with. I give them to you freely.

You are a Collector and so have the abilities to do just that. I wish, my dear, I could explain what you desire to know, but time is not on our side. You must go now. Do not worry. Gelmir and I will catch up with you." Leaning forward, she placed a kiss on the exact spot where she had transferred the information just moments before.

I watched as she turned away, moving to the door where Gelmir and I sat crouched on the floor. Gelmir had been watching the exchange as well, and when Emily moved to help him up, he spoke to me again.

"Go to the homeland. You will find the help you need there. Mack will be able to get you as far as the Hills. The rest of the way you will be on your own. Be careful and don't trust anyone. Do you understand, Alessar?" Clutching his hands in the soft material of my t-shirt, he prayed with the last of his strength for our safe escape.

"Emily and I will join you, when it is safe." His eyes fixed on me. He gazed deeply and spoke with his mind of the urgency with which we needed to go, "Protect her, Alessar. We need her more than you could ever know." Pushing away and breaking the link between us, he shouted, "Now go!"

I grabbed the backpack Emily had packed and flung it over my shoulder. Moving past Emily, who was now standing next to Dylan, I grabbed the young girl by the arm and pushed her out the door.

"Wait, I don't understand. What's happening; why are we leaving them behind?" Dylan screeched, as I dragged her from the house and down the steps to the back yard.

"There is no time for explanations; we need to move, and we need to do so now if we are to survive." Grabbing her by the shoulders, I swung her around and moved her in the direction we needed to go.

I felt the response to my harsh words grow into the steel that now showed in her spine. She was magnificent to look at, all-powerful and in control. Then, as if a giant weight was pressing down on her, she lost it completely. She was out of control. A little heady from the emotions that rolled off her, I shook my head and cleared her thoughts from my mind. What the hell was happening with her? Didn't she realize the danger we are in? I could sense her thoughts were all over the place and she was barely able to control her feelings. Now was not the time for a breakdown. Forcing her to move forward, I was shocked when she pulled her arm from my grip.

"I'm not going anywhere with you!" Snatching back her composure and gaining a little strength from the attitude that I had giving her, she seethed at my comments.

"Look here, little girl, if you want to ever see daylight again, you will listen to what I am saying, and you will high tail your tight little ass over that fence and down the road as quickly as possible!"

"Okay, I get that you are in a hurry. But could you possibly tell me who we are running from and why you think that they—whoever they are—are trying to hurt me?"

Seeing that I was getting nowhere with her, I decided to take the path of least resistance and show her what could happen if she didn't move her ass. Grabbing her hand in mine, I placed it on my chest and spoke to her using only the memories of my past to motivate her.

Pictures of war, memories of battle and death flashed before her eyes. I could feel her cringed at the sight of me covered in blood and riddled with pain on the battlefield. It was horrific! I was showing her what could happen if we delayed any longer, and that scared her more than anything. I watched as she slipped into a trance, no longer seeing what I was showing her. She had been taken away by a power who was gaining strength. Golda had come.

Dylan was aware of her. I watched as Golda showed herself to Dylan, attempting to push away the fear I had shown her. She dressed herself in white, fawning innocence, with her golden hair cascading down her back. She was beautiful, and I knew I had to do something that would get her back. Reaching out, I slapped her. She swayed with the strength of my hit. I felt the painful sting on her face, through the heat coming from my hand. There would be no mistaking what just happened.

"What the hell are you doing? Did you just slap me?" she screamed.

"Sorry about that, sweetheart. Golda was too close, and I needed you with me, not her." I moved away from her, feeling a little bit smug with the results of my actions. I was slipping through the fence line and starting to run down the back alley, when she finally came after me.

"Hey! What kind of jerk are you? You think you can just slap me and then take off?" She was upset and I understood that. With her anger pushing her, she followed my footsteps and quickly caught up with me.

"I think that I am the jerk Gelmir has put in charge of taking care of you, and you are the spoiled brat who keeps making my job so difficult." Picking up speed, I moved deftly though the back allies of the small town. "I need you to stop bitching right now, okay?"

I could sense that I had offended her. She began to say something in rebuttal to me when I felt Golda's presence. Knowing I had to do something quickly, I abruptly stopped. Whipping around, I placed my hand over her mouth. It wasn't enough. Golda would be able to feel her anger and feed from it. I needed to distract her. A split second passed before I made my decision. Removing my hand, I replaced it with my mouth.

Shocked at the heat moving though her, I completely absorbed every inch of her body. Flowing with a mind of its own, my body enveloped hers, wrapping her in its warming glow, from head to toe. Her entire being was flushed in heat, and I wanted more. She felt like nothing I had ever experienced before. She conquered every sense I had, bringing me to a complete boil, with only the gentle touch of her lips to mine.

I sensed her need. She wanted more, needed more. Clasping her hands in my hair, she pulled me closer and kissed even harder. Moving her body against mine and imploring me to do the same. Heat radiated from our entwined bodies. Kiss after kiss, moving her deeper with desire, I could feel her body taking in all I had to offer. And then as quickly as it had begun, I knew I had to stop.

Moving away from her, I watched as she gasped for air. She was standing on legs that reminded me of a newborn calf, wobbly and unsure. Slowly, she opened her eyes and I watched as the desire we shared in our embrace grew. I had to stop it. I had to make her see the need for swiftness, and anger was my best weapon.

"If you have had enough, I think we should keep moving!" I turned back and strode in the direction I had started. Hoping that my harsh words would anger her, shifting her into motion, I pressed on. "Move it, little girl, we have to hurry. We don't have time for make-out sessions." My false anger was puzzling to her. I could see it in her eyes. She wanted to ask the question that hovered, just on the tip of her tongue. "Why did you kiss me, then?" But, she didn't. Keeping her in the dark was necessary to fuel her anger.

I had kissed her in the beginning to hide from Golda. Somewhere along the way it had changed. She only followed along because I had shocked and surprised her with my actions. That is what I was telling myself, but I knew it was more than that. I knew how I made her feel and the knowledge of that just about did me in.

Glancing back at her again, I could see the wheels turning in her head. She was trying to figure out what to do next, her mind warring with herself. I could almost hear the argument going on in her head. "Who the hell does he think he is? Talk about gall. I never asked to make out with him. What nerve! The arrogant ass." Her thoughts were so strong I knew that, given the chance, she was going to point that out as soon as she caught up.

However, catching up with me would prove easier said than done. I was rather fast when I needed to be. I kept her at a safe distance, making it difficult for her to verbally start chewing me out for being so disrespectful to her, while pushing the need for speed. I was moving at a quick speed and she was gaining.

She had just gotten close enough to me to say something, when we both saw Mack and realized where we were. In only a matter of a few minutes, we had completely crossed town and were standing in front of Mack's old shop.

Seeing Mack had cooled her temper some. I watched as she stepped to where he stood and began speaking.

"Mack! Hey, I wanted to talk to you and—." Her words were cut off by Mack reaching out and pulling her into a huge bear hug before she could finish her sentence.

"No time, baby girl; we have to get you out of here right now!" Briskly letting go of her, he turned to me and, without saying another word, acknowledged the desperateness of the situation. I entered the garage and walked to its far corner to wait for him.

"Hurry, Mack! We have little time, and any head start you can give us will be greatly appreciated." Remembering the small satchel inside the pickup, I went to collect it. Reaching into the cab, I pulled out a few things I thought would be helpful and placed them all into the backpack Emily had given to me at the house. Directing my attention to Mack, I spoke.

"They are closer than I thought; I felt their presence just a few moments ago. They are headed to the house.

Emily and Gelmir will keep them busy until we can safely travel to our destination. Are you ready?"

Nodding his head, Mack responded, "I can only take one of you at a time, and the farthest I can get you to is the Hills. Once there, you will be on your own." I watched as he turned to Dylan and looked deep into her eyes. "I'm sorry, baby girl; one day I will explain. But for now, trust that I'm doing what's best for you and all you love." Grabbing hold of her waist and pulling her into his arms, he said a few words I didn't understand. Then light filled my eyes and they were gone.

Dylan

I was swimming, no floating, suspended in nothingness. Then there was light, a tunnel lit by hundreds of bright lights, speeding past me one after the other. It was as if I was on a rollercoaster ride of illumination. Beautiful at first, and then unable to take in the speed with which I was seeing the light, horrible. It was making me feel queasy and risking the contents of my stomach to come up. I covered my mouth, and prayed for strength to hold on, when abruptly it stopped.

Mack was still holding me, balancing my weight and steadying my stance. I heard him say something to me again and then he was gone. In a flash of light he disappeared. I tried to grasp his words to me, but the rolling in my stomach was too much. Falling to my knees, I heaved, holding my sides as the strain of the convulsion emptied the contents of my stomach onto the grass-covered ground.

Gaining some composure, I pulled myself to my feet and took in my surroundings. I was standing in the middle of what looked to be a forest. Trees surrounded me at every turn. Then it hit me, I was alone. Mack wasn't there and neither was the man named Alessar.

"Mack!" Hollering his name proved no results. Turning around again and again, I scoured my surroundings, looking for any sign of him. I saw nothing. He had completely disappeared. I felt the panic bubbling up inside me. I struggled to remember what Mack had said to me before I fell to my knees and unloaded my stomach onto the grass.

I was contemplating venturing a little farther into the trees in search of him, when another flash of light appeared just to the right of me. Turning to the light, I heard a soft thud and then Mack's voice.

"Dylan, baby girl, I need your help." Mack was holding Alessar in his arms, and it was obvious the man was unconscious. He was also covered in blood, a lot of blood; it took every ounce of my will not to unload my stomach for the second time. I watched, frozen in place as Mack slowly laid the limp body of Alessar to the ground. He grabbed the backpack that was still slung onto Alessar's back and removed it, placing it under his head and motioning for me to help him.

"Baby girl, I need you to stay here with him for just a moment. I will be right back." Mack stood up from the ground and moved to leave. He stopped when he realized

I had not moved an inch from where I had been standing before when he reappeared, carrying his unconscious load. Walking to where I stood frozen in place, overwhelmed at what I was seeing, he grabbed my shoulders gently and squeezed.

"Dylan, I need you to look after Alessar for just a moment. I will be right back and then I will explain. Do you understand, Dylan?" I could hear him talking, but I didn't comprehend what was happening. I was in shock. Grabbing my shoulders, he shook me and pleaded with me to come back to him.

"Dylan, snap out of it! I need you, now!" It was as if a light bulb went off inside of me. I cleared my thoughts and a strength that I didn't know I possessed came though. Finding my voice, I squeaked out a reply.

"Okay." A little sluggish at the sight of so much blood, I pleaded with my feet to move. Slowly at first, but then more rapidly when I finally gained back all my senses. I moved to sit next to the man, who just a few minutes before had kissed me like no other man had ever kissed me before.

Taking in his condition, I realized he might not have been as bad off as I had originally thought. It wasn't good, but it was a head wound and they tended to bleed more than most. I needed to stop the bleeding, so I could assess the damage and get a better idea of what I was dealing with.

"I need something to stop the bleeding." I said to Mack.

Mack was already removing his t-shirt and wadding it up into a ball before I could even finish the sentence. "Here, press this to the wound and watch his breathing. I will be right back." No sooner was the t-shirt in my hand than Mack turned and left, disappearing into the woods.

I knelt and applied the t-shirt to Alessar's wound. Alone again, with the exception of the man that lay bleeding and unconscious on the ground before me, I took stock in what had just happened.

Making sure that my newly acquired patient was breathing and the flow of blood from his head wound was slowing down, I felt comfortable absorbing my surroundings once again.

Disoriented at first and not completely aware of just where I was, I visually cataloged every detail as quickly as possible. We were in a forest, but which one? The trip here had been quite different, unlike any trip before. Miles had been traveled in a short period of time. That much was sure; there were no forests near the reservation, from which we had come. The closest was the Black Hills National Forest, over hundred miles away. But how had we gotten here? That was the question.

Racking my brain, I went over every detail of my environment and then began deciphering the past couple of days. Not that it was too terribly surprising, being somewhere completely unknown and getting there so quickly. The events of the morning had already been a very eye-opening experience. Digging into the memories Gelmir had shared with me, I determined that we had warp traveled to this place, wherever it was. But the unbelievable part was that it was Mack who had taken us.

With Gelmir opening up and sharing, there were fewer questions that needed answers. However, Mack and his unknown powers were almost more than I could handle.

What did he have to do with what was going on? How exactly did he fit into this puzzle that was being created before my very eyes? He was obviously an Immortal as well; who was he? Was he still the man who I thought I had known for so many years; or was he wearing a disguise, like Mrs. T, "Emily?" Was my entire childhood around him fake too—a show, a ruse to keep his baby girl subdued and unaware of my true identity?

My blood began to boil throughout my body, and the nausea that had once filled my senses completely disappeared, replaced with anger.

I barely noticed when Mack returned due to the anger that seething through my entire being. I only stepped aside when he nudged me away, allowing him to minister to the unconscious man lying on the bloodstained ground.

Stepping back farther, I watched as he placed a yellowish green poultice to the head wound and bandaged the wound completely. Once finished, he placed his hands over the wound and gently whispered words I didn't understand. Straining my ears to hear, I listened to what seemed to be a prayer in a language I was unfamiliar with. It was soothing, comforting the rage that had consumed me only moments before. With his words alone, he removed some of my anger and replaced it with warmth and compassion, almost as if his words had drugged me into feeling calmer.

Removing his hands from his patient, he stepped to where I stood. "Dylan, there is no time to explain; I will tell you all when the time is right." Leaning forward, he wrapped his arms around me and enveloped my small body in a bear hug.

"I don't understand what's happening." Shaking my head as I pushed him away, I said, "Who the hell are you, and how the hell did we get here?"

"I wish I had time to explain, but the longer I stay here, the easier it will become for Golda to find you." Moving to where the backpack lay on the ground next to the sleeping Alessar, he reached inside and pulled out a book.

"Here, read this. Understand that what you find inside will explain very little. Know that I am still the same person I have always been, your friend and loving Mack." Thrusting the book forward, he hurriedly returned to the ground next to the backpack, where he picked up the remains of the poultice he had placed on Alessar's wound and handed it to me. He explained as he did so that I would need to keep the wound clean and change the bandage once again before moving on in the next two hours.

"It's not safe here; Golda is strong. Gelmir is keeping her busy for now; but eventually she will come for you, and you don't want to be here when she does." Quickly he moved from the ground to where she stood. Grasping her once again, he framed her face with his hands. "Baby girl, if there was any way I could stay, I would, but I have to go. Gelmir and Emily need my help."

Holding my face and staring into my eyes, the pain that was there was almost unbearable. The unknown was sinking into every ounce of my body. Unsure and reasonably stricken with guilt, I watched as his eyes began to well with tears. The sight of Mack on the verge of weeping almost destroyed me.

Mentally praying and willing myself not cry, I turned from him and began to gather the things he had pulled from the backpack in his haste.

"I'm afraid if I don't go back now, it may be too late." Gaining strength by looking to the man lying on the ground, Mack pushed back the fear in his eyes. I watched as he stiffened his spine and listened as he lectured me like he had so many times in the past. It was comforting, and the strength he was showing me was just the new foundation I needed.

"Give him a chance, baby girl. He is a good man, and he will protect you with his own life." With firmness in his voice, he stepped away from me. Knowing that he was going to leave me soon, a slight bit of panic bubbled up.

"Wait, don't go! I'm not sure I understand what is happening here with all this." I waved my hands in the air, showing him my confusion. "Now there is this." I pointed a finger to the prone and wounded body of Alessar. "I don't know what I am doing, I am no nurse. He needs medical attention. You can't just leave us here." I squawked out as quickly as possible, hoping he would take pity on me and stay.

Shaking his head, he sighed and took hold of my hand. "Baby girl, you can do this. You are smart, strong, and more willful than anyone I have ever met. If anyone has the strength ingrained in them, it's you. Turn to what you know. It has always been there inside of you." He reached forward and placed his hand over my heart. "You are much stronger than you know, and with a little time, you will understand. Trust in yourself, trust in Alessar, and we will be reunited soon, I promise."

Feeling like a small child, insecure and unsure of everything, I whimpered, "I'm scared."

"I know. I am too. It's only natural; a lot has happened, and more is to come. But remember who you are and all will be well." He hugged me tightly once again, only to set me back so quickly that I lost a little balance and almost stumbled before getting a hold of myself and watching him go. It was quick—he was there, and then in a flash of light, he was gone.

"God help me!" I prayed as I walked to where Alessar lay unmoving on the ground. Sitting down to watch over him, I began thinking about the fact that I had said more prayers in the last forty-eight hours than I had in quite some time. Maybe now was a good time to say another.

Sixteen

Mack

"Where is she, Gelmir?" I could hear the interrogation as I entered the back of Emily's house. I had traveled back as quickly as possible, knowing that the dark Immortal, Golda, was battling Emily and Gelmir.

After depositing Dylan safely in the Hills, I had traveled back to the garage to get Alessar and discovered he wasn't there. Knowing the warrior would never leave his post willingly I ran to where I knew Gelmir and Emily would be.

Upon entering the backyard, I could see that Alessar was lying unconscious and bleeding, just to the side of the little red shed. Scorch marks on the ground were more than enough evidence to understand the warrior had been hit with bolt of energy so hard that it left him completely comatose.

I quickly grabbed the lifeless body and traveled to where I'd left my baby girl, over one hundred miles away in the Black Hills.

After treating Alessar's wounds, making sure that he would survive and being somewhat sure that Dylan would be okay, I traveled back to help Gelmir and Emily.

Slowly I crept through the back yard and up the steps to Emily's back door, avoiding the warrior who stood guard not twenty feet away.

Once I gained access to the house, I could hear Gelmir and Golda speaking. Scanning the room, it was obvious that they had been looking for something or someone. After hearing Golda's screeching voice raised in protest to Gelmir's unwillingness to be helpful, I was extremely glad to have gotten Dylan away when I did.

Golda was powerful. I could feel her energy all around me, as if I was inside one of those static balls, constantly moving with energy.

Gathering strength, I willed myself to take in my surroundings. The kitchen was in bad shape; they had obviously been in there when their fighting began. The walls, cabinets, and countertops still smoldered with heat, due to a direct hit from Golda's ability with fire.

I knew Golda had several abilities. I didn't know all that she was capable of, but I had seen some of the carnage that she had left behind when I had been a young boy, before coming to live on the rez.

She was pure evil, and I was having a difficult time figuring out how the hell I, a half-breed Immortal, was going to battle such a powerful Dark Lord. I had only just discovered my ability a few years ago, and it had taken me a long time to perfect it as much as I had.

I had all the regular Immortal strengths, but my true gift was that of travel. I could shift through time and travel anyplace I wanted, if I had been there before. Emily had been helping me for the past few years, enhancing my gift and gaining more ground every day. When I first began, I could travel from my house to the garage, just with a little blink of my eyes. Over time, the distances had gotten longer and my strength in shifting not just myself, but another person with me, had grown as well.

Crouching low next to the overturned table, I listened to what was being said in the living room, which was just out of my line of sight.

"Gelmir, you amaze me. You still fight well, but it has definitely taken its toll on you, hasn't it?" Laughing, Golda continued, "You're looking rather worn, my dear man."

She was mocking him, while throwing out energy to constantly keep him busy fighting. My senses were so alert I could feel the pain coming from both Gelmir and Emily, but I was at a loss as to what to do.

I had to figure out how to get in and out without being caught; but how? She would eventually sense my presence, and when she did, it would be all over for me.

"Golda, do you really think that I can't beat you? Your arrogance has always been your downfall; that is why you are so easy to beat," Gelmir said.

I could tell that Gelmir's last comment had struck a nerve in Golda. She retaliated with a stronger burst of energy that ripped pain through my entire body and was making it difficult to continue hiding and not just run.

Then Gelmir's voice came to me, "Mack, I need you. I cannot hold on much longer. I have Emily with me; come to me and travel quickly." Understanding what I needed to do, I slowly rose from my crouched position and willed myself the strength to move. A vision from Gelmir showed the interior of the living room and where he and Emily were standing, as well as where Golda and her warrior were.

My time was almost up. I could feel Gelmir weakening, and I needed to move fast. Pulling myself together, I said a quick prayer to the gods and readied myself for battle. Gelmir came to me one last time, "Now, Mack, *now!*"

I raced through the kitchen before Golda knew what was happening and grabbed Gelmir's shoulder; we swiftly moved though time. I knew I couldn't take the risk of exposing Dylan and Alessar, so I shifted time in the opposite direction and placed us in the middle of the Badlands, away from Golda and her dark arts and farther away from my baby girl and Alessar.

In the new location, I calmed my nerves and began taking a mental inventory on all that I had heard while waiting for the best opportunity to help Gelmir and Emily. Only then did I notice the white cat that was lying in Gelmir's hands and the fact that Emily was nowhere to be seen.

"Oh, my God, Emily! Where is she? Did we lose her?" Panic began to take over in my mind. I lost all sense of what was happening, until the white cat shifted in Gelmir's hands and began to transform.

"Mack, it is all right. I am here. Gelmir and I thought it would be easier to travel, with him so depleted of energy and unable to help much, if I shifted into a smaller mass." She stepped to me and touched my shoulder to comfort my worries.

"But we must hurry. Gelmir can no longer battle, and we need to get farther away than this." She quickly moved around to where Gelmir was still standing and grabbed his arms, pleading with him to sit.

"Gelmir, please, sit before you fall." Gently she guided him to a large embankment and settled him on the ground next to it. Looking at Mack, she continued, "You must go and get help; I'll stay with Gelmir and watch over him." She continued on, while checking Gelmir's forehead with the back of her hand, "He's running a slight fever and is very weak. I think he will be okay if he has a little rest before we move on."

I watched as Emily nursed Gelmir. Taking in my surroundings, I knew where we were. "We are close to the Anders Ranch. I'll find help there." Walking to where both Emily and Gelmir now sat on the ground, I knelt and placed my hand on Emily's shoulder. "I will run to the Anders Ranch and get help. I shouldn't be gone long. Make sure to keep him out of the sun as much as you can."

"Hurry, Mack! He needs to see a healer, and I am afraid that if we don't get to one soon…" Her words faded away. She was afraid to say what she was thinking, but I knew. Gelmir was dying; it was obvious.

Gelmir was unable to speak, and the strength that he had used during battle with Golda had left him so fragile that I was afraid to leave him.

Still kneeling beside Emily, I stroked her back and comforted her as much as I could, "Don't worry; I'll get help, Emily. Together we will get him to a healer. Gelmir is stronger that you think; he will pull through this."

Standing, I moved to leave, but not before squeezing Emily's shoulder and willing her what little strength I had left. "I'll be back." I ran in the direction of the Anders ranch, but before I was completely out of sight, I looked back one last time, praying to the gods to protect them. It would be the last time I would ever see Emily and Gelmir together on the reservation, and it would be the beginning of my new life as a lost Immortal.

Keep watching for the next installment of the Immortals Lost entitled *Dark Days*.

Read an excerpt from the journal of Gelmir.

Gelmir
Journal entry 8–12–2009

It is a new beginning, the gathering has begun. Those who believe in peace and the survival of our kind are assembling, preparing for what will be the future of our species and the long anticipated return of the Creators.

The Chosen One is among us now. The Seers have predicted her arrival. Our day of peace among the races draws near. But I fear that battle is closer to the horizon than the elders understand and so I continue to search.

As an elder of the Immortal Prime, it's my responsibility to find the lost. Many years ago during the time of the great wars, young Immortals were forgotten or misplaced.

It was a necessity at the time. I fear a necessity that may have been made in vain.

This world we live in is one of secrecy. We hide for fear of being found and destroyed. Not only by those who wish to gain control but also by those who do not understand. The fear of the unknown spurs all who are afraid into making bad decisions. These decisions can and will affect all of us, both mortal and immortal.

It is my fear that the secrecy and the protection of our world's ways has brought us much despair. Our younger generation has suffered greatly. Most have been lost to us for centuries, completely unaware of who and what they really are.

Not only do our young suffer, so do the human race and their understanding of our species. The humans grow to hate our powers and us. Where we once stood together, we are now separated by our differences.

We have lost many. Entrusted to the hands of both mortal and immortals, only to be lost in the battle with darkness or forgotten completely. Have we failed?

The original twelve, those left behind so many centuries ago, now dwindle in strength and numbers. They were the first charged with the responsibility and understanding that darkness would not succeed in their domination of this planet without a fight. Only four of us are left standing, and we struggle to continue.

My strength grows weaker every day. I once believed, in the beginning, that we were successful against the darkness. I am now seeing the error in that judgment.

We have fallen short of our responsibilities. The younger generation has been lost or misplaced, and the darkness continues to grow.

We may have stopped the carnage in the past, centuries ago, but we have lost much hope of succeeding in the future.

It is in the strength of my constant companion, Alessar, that I hold any hope of success. Every day he shows great strength, giving me hope where little remains. We continue *to search for the lost, hoping we can guide them to their true identity before shadow and evil finds them and takes them away to a darkness few escape.*

I pray that I will be able to withstand the darkness when it comes for me again. And it will come, of that much I am sure.

The Chosen One is among us. I feel her presence at times, but without help to search for her, I fear the strength of our enemy will overcome us.

It is a race against time, a battle that we cannot afford to lose. With her identity unknown to both sides, she is hunted.

The Seers have given us a clue. The one carrying the mark of the promised will know her identity. Only she will see the Chosen One for who she is and only then will the keys come together and the creators be summoned.

The Chosen will be found eventually, and those who do the finding will be the victors in this battle amongst brothers.

Our only hope lies in the lost Immortals who continue to gather for the good of all races.

Look for the thrilling sequel from H.R. Phillips